TEODORA KOSTOVA

Thank you.
Love,
Teodora :)

Copyright@ Teodora Kostova 2016

ISBN-13: 978-1540394323

ISBN-10: 1540394328

All right reserved. No reproduction, copy or transmission of this publication may be made without written permission of the author. No paragraph of this publication may be reproduced, copied or transmitted without the written permission of the author.

Edited by Kameron Mitchell
Proofread by Vicki Potter and Jennifer Reilley
Cover art by Jay Aheer at Simply Defined Art

Disclaimer

This is a work of fiction. All names, places and incidents are either the product of the author's imagination, or are used fictitiously.

KISS AND RIDE

December

"Hold the door!" Someone shouted in English, startling Luca into action. But before he could reach the button, an arm pushed between the rapidly closing elevator doors.

Luca's heart skipped a beat; he knew there was a sensor that would stop the doors from closing and crushing every bone in the man's arm, but it still felt surreal to see the huge metal doors closing in on the thin arm. Like jaws about to have their meal. Or maybe he was so fucking tired from the ten hour flight he'd worked that his brain was turning to mush.

"Ugh," the man grunted as the doors opened and he stepped into the elevator, pulling a small suitcase behind him. Casting a look in Luca's direction, the man didn't offer any greeting. Instead, he draped the black wool coat he was carrying over the suitcase and leaned back against the wall, closing his eyes as the doors dinged closed.

Luca stared at the guy. He was about an inch shorter than Luca's own five-foot-nine, but unlike Luca he didn't pack any bulk at all. His jeans hugged his slender frame enticingly, his t-shirt hung loose under the grey cardigan he wore. The thin cotton scarf draped around his neck and the high-top Converse on his feet completed the guy's perfectly styled, yet casual, outfit.

As the elevator descended, the guy kept his eyes closed, but his expression was anything but relaxed. There was a deep crease between his prominent black eyebrows, and his wide mouth was set into a thin, pale line. A few curls of his thick hair had escaped the loose knot on the back of his head and were framing his face in a way that softened the sharp lines of his jaw and cheekbones. Numerous silver piercings in different shapes adorned both his ears, and Luca squinted to try and see what they were.

"Quit staring," the guy said without even opening his eyes.

Embarrassed heat flooded Luca's body, making him blush furiously.

What the fuck was wrong with him? Ogling a hot guy like some creep? Blushing like a teenager caught staring at dirty magazines?

Get a fucking grip, Romano.

Luca cleared his throat. "Sorry. I didn't mean to. I'm just tired and my social skills are lacking, I'm afraid."

KISS AND RIDE

He offered a tentative smile when the guy blinked his eyes open at him. They were a gorgeous deep blue, but as he watched him under heavy lids, Luca noticed the dark circles around them and the redness dimming their sparkle.

The guy opened his mouth to say something, but just then the lights flickered and the elevator came to an abrupt halt. The lights went out, and the sudden darkness was as startling as it was suffocating.

"You've got to be fucking kidding me!" The guy said, his voice low, but he sounded tired more than angry. As if this was the last drop of unfortunate events he'd endured recently.

"Don't worry," Luca rushed to say. "There's emergency lighting that should come on..." The small light on the ceiling flickered to life, casting a bluish light over them. "Any moment," Luca added with a smile.

"Great. Just fucking great." The guy slumped to the floor, dropping his head in his palms.

"Hey," Luca said softly, taking the small step separating them and sitting on the floor next to the guy. He radiated misery like a beacon, and for some reason Luca's heart ached for him. The need to comfort him was overwhelming, but considering he'd just met the guy, Luca wasn't sure how to go about it. Thankfully, he'd had extensive training how to deal with people when they were upset, scared, sick, or simply being assholes, so he was pretty sure he could handle anything. "I'm sure it's nothing serious and we'll be on our way down again in a few minutes."

The guy lifted his head, focusing his tired eyes on Luca. "We're caught in a box hanging several floors above the ground, and right now the mechanism operating said death trap is fucked. So don't tell me it's going to be okay. Any moment now we could be falling down to certain death."

Luca bit his lip. Even in the exhausted state he was in, he was still pretty sure laughing when someone stared at you with unguarded fear in their eyes was not polite.

"The mechanism operating the elevator is not fucked. There are safety locks in place in case of power outage. We may be stuck here until the power comes back on, or worst case scenario, until we're rescued, but this death trap is not falling down."

The worry etched on the guy's face started to melt away, his expression softening. He seemed so utterly defeated, and it tugged at Luca's heartstrings.

"How do you know so much about elevators?" The guy asked, surprising Luca.

"I got stuck in one years ago, freaked out like you did just now. Afterwards, I researched how elevators in modern buildings worked." Luca lifted one shoulder in a shrug, relaxing his posture.

"I didn't freak out," the guy mumbled, resting his head back against the wall. Luca's eyes were drawn to his throat, the pale skin as the Adam's apple bobbed,

KISS AND RIDE

the smooth shaven jaw, the dark beauty mark on his neck.

Luca averted his eyes, staring at the floor, embarrassed that he might be caught staring again.

"Are you a flight attendant?" the guy asked, jerking his chin towards Luca's uniform.

"*Si*," Luca said automatically. He spoke four languages fluently, but when he was tired his brain was slower to process the information, and more often than not, he ended up speaking in his native tongue, sometimes without even realizing it. "Yes," he corrected himself with an apologetic smile.

"S'alright," the guy waved him off. "We can talk in Italian if you prefer."

"You speak Italian?" Luca asked, surprised. The guy was obviously American, and judging by his accent Luca was pretty sure he was a New Yorker.

"*Si*," the guy said, and for the first time since he'd stormed into the elevator, he smiled. Luca couldn't look away from that smile. It reached the guy's tired eyes, and made his cheeks dimple, and transformed his whole face. He was beautiful anyway, all sharp angles and messy hair and intense eyes, but when he smiled he turned into this carefree creature that lured you in with his charm. "Both my parents were Italian, my mom was born in New York to Italian parents, and always spoke Italian to me. And my dad lived here, in Rome." The guy's Italian was flawless. It was nothing like the odd dialect Italian-Americans usually spoke.

Luca's mind flashed to the first time he'd been to New York, what seemed like ages ago, and thought he could go to Little Italy and speak freely in Italian with anyone there. How wrong he'd been. The strange mixture of Italian dialects and Americanisms New Yorkers of Italian descent used was nothing like the language spoken in Italy.

"You look surprised," the guy said with a cocky grin. "I told you I could speak Italian."

"I thought you meant New York Italian, not *Italian* Italian." Luca was surprised the guy could read him so well, considering they'd met five minutes ago. Usually he was the one good at reading people, at anticipating what they wanted before they even said it out loud.

"My mom insisted I learn to speak properly," he said, his smile dimming away from his eyes.

"You talk of your parents in past tense," Luca said, not really a question. The guy obviously had a lot on his plate right now, and sometimes talking to a complete stranger was better than sharing your troubles with friends and family.

"Mom passed away when I was fourteen," the guy said, resting his chin on his knees as he hugged his legs. The move was so child-like it made him look fourteen all over again, even if he seemed to be in his early twenties. "And my dad died two weeks ago." He swallowed thickly, then sighed. "I'm here for the memorial service."

KISS AND RIDE

God. No wonder the guy was wrecked.

"My condolences," Luca said softly, placing a hand on the guy's shoulder.

"Thanks." The word came out automatically, and more like an instinctive reply. The guy straightened his back, extended his legs in front of him and leaned his head against the wall, the angry frown returning. Luca dropped his hand. "I'm not sad or anything. I hated the guy."

Luca was taken aback by his words, mainly because they didn't match his body language. The man before him was devastated.

"Want to talk about it?" Luca asked tentatively. He didn't know how long they had until the power came back on, but the urge to comfort the beautiful, sad man was twisting uncomfortably in his gut.

"There isn't much to say. The asshole left when I was five, never to be seen again. When Mom died, social services tracked him down, but he refused to take me in. I was sent to foster care." The guy's voice was monotonous but it felt forced. As if he was doing his best not to show any emotion, as if all this had happened to someone else.

Luca wanted to know more. He wanted to know *why*. Who would do such a thing? Turn away their own child?

But he kept his mouth shut. The misery was pulsing off the guy once again and Luca didn't think poking around to satisfy his own curiosity was fair.

"I'm such an idiot." The guy folded his arms, then glared at the elevator door as if he'd forgotten Luca was even there. "He didn't want anything to do with me, and yet when he died I maxed out my credit card to get on the next flight here."

Luca wanted to say so many things. That he wasn't an idiot for loving his father even if he didn't love him back; that what he'd done was the right thing to do and it'd probably give him closure; that you couldn't help how you felt even if every rational cell in your brain told you it was wrong.

"And for what?" the guy continued, dropping his hands to the floor in defeat. "Everything that could go wrong did go wrong, and now I'm stuck in an elevator and will probably be late for the damn service, and it was all for nothing."

Luca's pulse sped up. "It's today?"

The guy nodded. "In about an hour."

They needed to get out of here. The desire to help the guy burned through Luca, and he was determined he wouldn't allow him to be late for his father's memorial service.

"Where?" Luca asked, standing up. He stepped closer to the buttons, looking for an emergency button or something. Did anyone even know they were stuck in here? The red emergency button on top of the panel remained mute however many times Luca pressed it.

"In Santa Maria di Loreto."

KISS AND RIDE

Fuck. That was in the historic center, and traffic there was always heavy. Luca's apartment was a ten minute drive from the church, so he knew the route well, and any shortcuts they could use, but still. They were trapped in Air Italia Tower, the brand new luxurious building right next to Fiumicino airport, designed to help tourists get rid of any remaining Euros in the array of stores and restaurants, and then give their credit cards a work-out in the five star hotel and spa on the top six floors.

The guy banged his head against the wall in a gesture of utter frustration and defeat. Just then, as if activated by him, the lights in the elevator came to life and they were suddenly moving again.

"See?" Luca beamed at him. "Told you it wouldn't be long before it was fixed."

Irrational joy that his companion wouldn't be late to say goodbye to his father bloomed in his chest. Reaching an arm towards the guy on the floor, Luca helped him up when he caught his hand, and on an impulse, straightened the shoulders of his cardigan, and fixed his scarf.

"You're going to be just fine, *amico*."

The guy stared at him with wide, red-rimmed eyes, his lips slightly parted as if he was in a daze, but he managed a slight nod.

TEODORA KOSTOVA

Outside, it was pouring.

Of course it was. Vin wouldn't expect the universe to suddenly take pity on him. Vaguely, he wondered what else could go wrong in the next half an hour, preventing him from going to his dad's memorial service after all.

"Fuck," he swore, suddenly remembering he'd spent all his cash in Euros at the bar as he tried to calm his fucking nerves. The guy he'd met in the elevator, who he'd stupidly spilled his sob story to, stopped and turned to look at him, propping his suitcase upright. He looked sharp in his uniform – a navy suit that looked as if it was tailored for him – and not a single crease in sight. The coat he shrugged on was black and seemed way too warm for the mild weather in Rome. "Can I exchange money anywhere around here?"

The guy didn't immediately respond as if mentally going through all the stores and services offered at the Air Italia Tower. Vin took the opportunity to study him, the light of day and the open space making his features sharper than what they'd seemed in the elevator. His dark eyes were framed with the thickest lashes Vin had ever seen, and when they focused on him Vin couldn't help the thrilling shiver that ran down his body. For a fleeting second he let himself imagine what that neatly trimmed beard would feel like on his skin, and how the guy's immaculately styled short hair would look in the morning.

When the guy didn't say anything for a long moment, staring at Vin as if seeing right inside his soul, Vin cleared his throat and asked, "Do cabs here take credit cards?" His heart sped up at the question, taking him out of his lustful stupor, and reminding him why he was here in the first place.

"Come on," was all the guy said, waving Vin to follow him as he turned on his heel and walked away from the curb.

"Wait, what?" Vin grabbed the handle of his suitcase and jogged after him. "Where are we going?"

The guy stopped and turned, making Vin halt mid step.

"I'm going to give you a ride to the basilica. My car is parked in the underground parking lot." He started walking again, not giving Vin a chance to protest.

He did anyway. "But, why?" Vin fell in step with the guy, finding himself following him without any logical explanation why. He was sure he could easily find somewhere to exchange his dollars back inside, or at the very least, the cabs should accept credit cards, shouldn't they?

"Because I don't want you to be late for your father's memorial service."

"But you just met me."

The guy slowed his pace, his brows creasing in confusion. "So?"

Ah, the famous Italian hospitality. Vin had always been a little uncomfortable with how affectionate, how intimate Italians always acted with each other, even if they'd just met. But he'd learned to accept that as a character trait he obviously hadn't inherited.

"You don't even know my name," Vin tried again. The guy kept walking, but Vin could see a smile curving his lips.

"What's your name?" He asked, turning to Vin.

"It's Vin. Short for Vincent, but Vin is fine."

"Nice to meet you, Vin." The guy extended his hand. When Vin took it, he squeezed his palm in a firm handshake. "I'm Luca." Vin smiled as he nodded. "Are we sufficiently acquainted now?" Vin nodded again, releasing Luca's hand. "Good. Let's go. Traffic at this time of the day is a nightmare."

KISS AND RIDE

Luca drove his tiny Fiat 500 – pearl white with the Italian flag stripes on the hood and roof – like a maniac. Vin clutched at the arm rest, his foot pressing on an imaginary break, all the while trying not to throw up. The other drivers were no better – sharply weaving through traffic without indicating, breaking at the last possible moment, and treating the red light more as a suggestion than the law.

In Manhattan traffic was always bad, but he could pretty much cross a road with his eyes closed, and cars would stop to avoid hitting him. They would honk at him, drivers would lean out the window and swear at him in all kinds of languages, but they would at least try and avoid turning him into roadkill.

The Romans didn't seem to be so considerate. In the fifteen minutes spent in the car, Vin had witnessed vehicles not even reducing their speed as they cut red lights at pedestrian crossings, barely avoiding running people over.

"What kind of madness is this?" Vin asked, watching horrified as one of the many scooters he'd seen that day sped through a busy zebra crossing without a moment's hesitation.

"Asks the New Yorker," Luca said with a snort. Just as Vin opened his mouth to explain that yes, traffic in New York was awful but at least he didn't fear for his life every time he set foot on the street, Luca added. "You've never been to Rome before?"

"No. I was never invited to visit. Not that I wanted to." Vin slumped in his seat, the anger he felt towards his father reigniting.

It never actually left him, the anger. It simmered below the surface of his skin ever since he could remember, roaring to life with the slightest nudge, then calming, but always there. Always burning.

Thinking about it, Vin couldn't imagine who he would be without it. It had defined him his whole life, and now, out of nowhere, the big bad monster was gone and Vin had nobody to be angry with.

Luca didn't say anything else for the rest of the horrifying ride. Vin was thankful. His anxiety about his father's memorial service was reaching its peak, and he needed a few moments to try and collect himself before he faced... What would he face when he got to the church?

With a jolt of panic Vin realized he had no idea if his father had any family in Rome. Or friends. Hell, he might have gotten married and had a bunch of kids.

Palms sweating, Vin rubbed them on his thighs, the thought of meeting any of his father's relatives or – god forbid – his own half brothers and sisters, terrified him. Why hadn't he thought this through? The man had abandoned him, twice, and yet Vin's first instinct when the lawyer had contacted him had been to max out his credit card and buy a plane ticket to Rome.

"Hey," Luca said, his voice gently extracting Vin from his self-induced panic attack. "Are you

KISS AND RIDE

feeling alright? You look like you're going to throw up."

Luca had parked the car right in front of the church, and was studying Vin critically, half turned in the driver's seat, hand on the wheel. Vin hadn't even noticed they'd stopped moving.

"I don't think I'm going to throw up," Vin said, leaning back in the seat, counting his breaths, trying to calm down. "But I don't think I can do this."

God, he was being such a loser. Sitting in this guy's car, freaking out and on the verge of tears. They'd met five minutes ago. Luca didn't need this drama. They were practically strangers.

"I'm sorry," Vin said, rubbing a hand over his face. "I'll be out of your hair in a minute. Just give me a sec, okay?"

Luca sighed loudly. Vin dared a glance in his direction, but instead of annoyed impatience, he saw Luca watching him with what could only be described as empathy.

"Come on," Luca said, opening the door and sliding out of the car.

Thankfully, the rain had stopped. Vin followed suit, fully expecting to be handed his suitcase and bid goodbye. On the sidewalk, Luca put his hands on Vin's shoulders and focused his dark eyes on him.

"I don't know what it's like to lose a parent," he said, his eyes glistening like onyx in a stream. "Not like that anyway. So I can only imagine what you're going through. And even if you insist you hated your dad, you still need to go in there and say your goodbyes, because you won't get another chance. Do it for you, not for him or anyone else. It may put your anger to rest, no?"

Vin didn't trust his voice to speak so he simply nodded. His gaze swept past Luca to the millions of twinkling lights decorating every building, lamp post and window. All different colors and shapes, they looked like stardust. The corners of Vin's mouth lifted as he imagined Tinkerbell going a bit crazy with the pixie dust, sprinkling it liberally over the whole of Rome until the Eternal City floated in the air like an enchanted island.

"Vin?" Luca's voice drew him back to reality.

"Yeah, you're right." Vin hated the prinkling behind his eyes. He wasn't going to cry on the streets of Rome, a few days before Christmas when you could actually feel the joy and peace in the air, in front of a stranger who probably thought Vin was a basket case by now.

"Is there anyone you know in there?"

Vin shook his head. "No. I have the name and vague description of the lawyer who called me, and he said he'd meet me here, but I don't know anyone else."

"Okay, let's go then." Luca let go of Vin's shoulders and turned towards the church.

"Where are you going?" Vin found himself once again jogging after Luca, completely unprepared for his reaction.

KISS AND RIDE

"I'm coming with you," Luca said, as if it was obvious.

"Why would you do that?" Vin stepped in front of Luca, cutting him off.

"For support." The 'duh' was left unsaid but it was evident in Luca's voice. He was staring at Vin as if *Vin* was the one acting crazy.

"You just met me," Vin insisted weakly. Truth be told, he really wanted Luca to go inside the church with him.

"Would you stop with that already? Why does it matter so much to you when we met?" Vin shrugged, not really having an answer to that question. "Fact is, we *did* meet. And I want to help you because something in those sad blue eyes of yours compels me to." Vin stared at him, rooted to the spot, not knowing what to say. "Look," Luca said, raking a hand through his hair, messing up the carefully styled locks. "If you want me to go, I'll go. But I figured you could use a friendly face in there."

He was right, of course. The thought of climbing those steps and entering the majestic basilica to face whatever awaited inside, all alone, terrified Vin.

"Okay," Vin said, taking a step sideways and turning to stand next to Luca. "Thanks."

Luca hummed in acknowledgement, and they started up the steps, side by side.

Vin thought his heart would beat out of his chest as they entered through the grand wooden doors. Inside, the air seemed to shrink, sucking all the oxygen out of his lungs. Luca placed a comforting hand on his upper arm and guided him further inside.

The first thing Vin saw as they entered was a large photo of his father propped on the pedestal behind the lavishly decorated altar. Antonio Alesi was smiling in it, showing a row of perfect white teeth, his cheeks dimpled, his blue eyes twinkling. His dark wavy hair was tucked behind his ears and he looked decades younger than his fifty years.

Vin had actually seen that same photo during one of his recent Google snooping sessions.

Walking down the aisle between the pews, Vin noticed the amount of people gathered. There was barely any space on the shiny wooden benches. The lawyer that had tracked Vin down last week had explained that Antonio'd wished for a private funeral with family only, and a separate memorial service for anyone else willing to pay their respects. The fact that Vin hadn't been invited to the funeral hung suspended between the words, a giant looming paper crane everyone pretended to ignore.

"Your dad was Antonio Alesi?" Luca whispered in his ear as they approached the front row.

"*Si*. Do you know him?"

"Everyone knows him! His work is in the *Galleria d'Arte Moderna*!"

Vin nodded but didn't say anything. It didn't seem like the best time to discuss his father's art. Of course he knew his dad was an incredibly talented artist – he'd inherited that fucking talent after all – and he knew he made a lot of money from the pieces he sold. Private collectors all over the world were making outrageous offers on his work, and some of his paintings and sculptures were exhibited in galleries of modern art all over the world.

None of that mattered to Vin. His dad's talent, fame, or money hadn't saved him from four years in foster care. They hadn't looked after his mother when she got cancer. They hadn't hugged him goodnight every night, or put on a Santa costume every Christmas, or wished him happy birthday every year.

They hadn't saved Antonio from the heart attack that had claimed his life.

"Vincent?" A soft voice said from the front row of the pews. Vin turned to see a middle-aged man with greying hair, friendly dark eyes, and wearing an impeccable black suit stand up and walk over to them. "Vincent Alesi?"

"Yes. That's me."

The man introduced himself as Lorenzo Donati, the lawyer who was handling Antonio's estate and had contacted Vin about the memorial service.

"You look just like your father," Lorenzo said affectionately, clasping Vin's outstretched hand in both of his.

Pleasantries were exchanged, introductions were made, and finally Vin and Luca were seated at the front row just as the priest took his place behind the altar. His speech seemed generic and Vin spaced out during most of it. He couldn't tear his eyes from the portrait of his dad. His face so familiar, so like Vin's, and yet so foreign.

People lined up to say a few words and pay their respects after the priest's official speech was done. Vin watched them, holding his breath before each and every one of them introduced themselves, fearing he'd have to deal with the revelation he had siblings he didn't know of, or some distant relatives who'd want to introduce themselves to him later on.

But that didn't happen. Everyone who spoke was either a colleague, or a former student from the Rome University of Fine Arts where Antonio used to teach a class for a while, or a friend. They all spoke fondly of him – affectionately – sharing amusing, uplifting stories about what a great man Antonio Alesi had been. And the whole time Vin's anger grew more intense at the pit of his stomach. It burned like a pool of lava, ready to erupt with the slightest provocation.

"Do you want to say a few words?" Lorenzo whispered in Vin's ear when the last person to speak was done.

Flick. Spark. Ignite.

"Sure." Vin stood up, glanced at Luca who was watching him warily, and walked to the podium in a trance. The blood was rushing in his ears, and his vision blurred around the edges, softening his focus. He felt drunk, even if he'd only had a couple of drinks hours ago.

All these people had known his father better than he ever had. All of them had interacted with him, some on a daily basis, and all of them seemed to think they had some claim on him just because he let them in their lives.

Well, tough shit. Vin was his *son*, his blood. His heir. The carbon copy of Antonio Alesi that not only smiled back at him in the mirror, but poured out of him in his art.

"Good afternoon," he began, stepping on the podium, thankful to his mother for insisting he speak flawless Italian. "My name's Vincent Alesi, and Antonio Alesi was my father." He paused for dramatic effect, expecting a collective gasp, pearl-clutching and wide-eyed stares, but got none of that. People simply observed him, some of them nodding as if they actually fucking knew who he was. "Most of you told beautiful stories of how generous, talented and charismatic my father was. And I appreciate that. I wish I'd known the person you all spoke of today. But I didn't." Vin felt his throat tighten and his eyes fill with tears, but dammit, he wasn't going to stop now. He needed to let go of all the frustration, anger, sadness, and sheer helplessness that was tearing him up inside. "Because he chose to leave me when I was a kid, never called or wrote or invited me to visit, and then turned me away when I needed him the most." He blinked slowly, letting the tears flow down his cheeks, looking at all the people gathered to honor his father, but seeing no one. "So all of your wonderful stories? They make no sense to me. To me Antonio Alesi was a cruel, selfish man whose only priority was his art."

From the corner of his eye he saw Luca stand up and move towards him, then felt more than saw an arm circling his shoulders, leading him away. Vin didn't resist. He had nothing left to fight with.

Vin didn't realize Luca was guiding him outside until the crisp December air hit his face. He'd left his coat inside, and so had Luca, so they huddled together against the massive wall of the basilica. When Vin rested his forehead on Luca's shoulder, Luca's arms enveloped him without hesitation.

In normal circumstances this would have probably been awkward as hell, seeking comfort from a guy he'd met a couple of hours ago. But after disgracing his father's memory in front of everyone who cared about him, Vin needed a break. He couldn't take back what he'd done, and in this moment he wasn't sure he wanted to. So many times he'd imagined flying to Rome, knocking on his father's door and pouring all his anger for the man right in his face, before storming away. But now? Now he'd never get a chance to do that, and what he'd just done seemed like the next best thing.

"Ai, *carino*," Luca murmured in his hair, his fingers massaging the back of his neck. "I'm so sorry."

KISS AND RIDE

Vin sniffled, then accepted the tissue Luca produced from his pocket. Hastily, he wiped his eyes, blew his nose, then stuffed the tissue in his back pocket. Luca was watching him, tracking his movements, his own eyes glazed over.

"I need to go back inside and apologize," Vin said, leaning a shoulder against the cold wall. Guilt replaced everything inside him, fluffy white foam falling on top of his anger and extinguishing it. "All these people loved and respected my father, and I acted like a brat."

"You said what was in your heart." Luca mimicked Vin, leaning against the wall and folding his arms.

"I should have dealt with my issues in private. It's not fair to them." Vin stabbed a finger towards the door of the church. "They didn't go through what I did, and everything I've seen and heard today leads me to believe my father was an asshole *only* to me."

Why?

That was the question Vin would never get to ask.

Luca placed a hand on Vin's forearm, squeezing gently. His dark eyes were kind, and so fucking deep Vin wanted to drown in them. For an endless moment, Vin was a captive, a willing victim, not even struggling to get away from the spell of Luca's intense gaze.

Vin lowered his lashes to Luca's mouth, the plump, perfectly bowed lips tempting him. They moved, forming his name, but Vin didn't look away. The need to feel these lips against his own surged through him, settling at the pit of his stomach.

"Vincent?" A female voice came right behind Luca, and Vin shifted his focus to the woman walking towards them.

They didn't jump apart when she reached them, only slightly moved away from each other, but the moment was broken. Something had shifted between them, though. Something big that Vin didn't feel like analyzing right now.

"Yes?" Vin said, straightening his shoulders, ready to face whatever accusations of inappropriate behaviour she was going to fling at him.

"I'm Maria Alesi, Antonio's sister." She smiled at him, tears shimmering behind her blue eyes. She looked a lot like his dad, only she was tiny, and very slender. Her dark curls fell to her shoulders in a stylish cut that framed her beautiful features. "I don't suppose you even knew you had an aunt?" Her voice was casual, but the sadness behind her eyes gave her away.

"I didn't."

Vin had no energy left to be angry anymore. He'd reached a point where he simply didn't care.

"Listen, I..." Maria began, faltering when she met Vin's unwavering, cold stare. "I'm here for you if you need to talk." She opened her purse, rummaging through it until she located whatever it was she needed. "I can see you're not ready to ask your questions yet, or rather, to hear the answers." She handed him a sleek business card with her name and phone number. Vin took it, more out of courtesy than anything else. He wasn't sure he'd ever want to talk to her, but he was done being rude to people today.

When he lifted his eyes back to Maria's, she was watching him with a sad smile, the tears in her eyes ready to spill.

"Ai, *bellissimo*," she said, a tear rolling down as she cupped his cheek with her warm hand. Something snapped inside Vin and he felt his own sadness bubble to the surface. The way this woman was looking at him as if he was the most precious thing in the world, broke him.

He could have had that. All these years, he could have had a family. He could have been loved.

"Call me anytime," Maria said, wiping a tear from his cheek before turning on her heel and walking briskly away.

"Fuck," Vin swore, extracting the used tissue and wiping his eyes again. "Is this fucking day ever gonna end?"

Luca pulled him in his arms and simply held him for a while. When he pulled away, he kept hold of his shoulders and said,

"God, you're a mess."

Vin laughed, a little too loudly, making him seem like a maniac. "Tell me something I don't know."

"Come on, let's go get our coats and get out of here."

The thought of going back into that church terrified Vin. His legs were frozen on the spot even when Luca started walking back towards the doors. Thankfully, Luca read his deer-in-the-headlights expression, and tossed him the car keys.

"Go sit in the car, I'll be right back."

"So," Luca said, closing the car door and reaching for the seatbelt. "Where to?"

Vin looked confused. Then, realization must have hit him because he closed his eyes and rested his head against the seat.

"Just leave me at the nearest hostel."

"Wait, what? You don't have a hotel reservation?"

"No," Vin said with a sigh, opening his eyes but not turning to face Luca. "Days before Christmas? Everything I could afford was fully booked. The only

KISS AND RIDE

rooms available were expensive suites in five star hotels."

Shocked into silence, Luca opened and closed his mouth a few times, but didn't say anything. Vin's head rolled on the seat, his eyes settling on him.

"Most hostels don't even advertise online. So I figured they wouldn't be too busy at Christmas when everyone wants a little luxury in their lives, and I could easily just show up somewhere and they'll have a room for me."

Luca still couldn't believe someone would jump on a plane across the ocean and not have a place to spend the night. But looking at Vin, he didn't seem too concerned. And in all honesty, he was probably right – if they went to a hostel right now they'd probably have a room or two available.

But the thought of Vin, all alone and drowning in his misery, on Christmas no less, made Luca's heart ache.

"We're going to my place," he announced, buckling his seatbelt and starting the engine.

"I can't let you do that," Vin said, only a shadow of his previous vigorous protests left in his voice. "You've done more than enough for me today. Just leave me at a hostel, I'll be fine."

"What if I don't want to?" Luca asked as he pulled out of the parking spot and merged into traffic.

"What do you mean?"

"I usually spend the holidays alone," Luca said, wondering how much he should say. He really didn't feel like talking about his family right now. Vin had enough problems of his own. "Not by choice. My parents and I are estranged, and it's been a long time since I actually dated someone beyond a casual hook-up." He glanced at Vin for a second to see him staring at his profile with a frown. Focusing his attention back on the road, Luca added, "You don't have anywhere to stay and I have a perfectly good couch. And we don't have to be alone on Christmas. We can cook dinner and watch Netflix, and you can help me decorate. It'll be fun and it doesn't have to be a big deal."

Vin was quiet, as if weighing Luca's words in his mind. It made Luca nervous. Had he come on too strong? He didn't mean to, but sometimes he did that and it threw people off.

"Look," Luca said, stopping at a red light and turning to face Vin. "I'm not coming on to you, I promise. I'd just love to share a meal with someone on Christmas."

"You're gay?" Vin asked.

The light turned green and Luca had to focus his attention back on the road, so he couldn't see Vin's reaction when he said,

"Yes. Is that an issue for you?" He couldn't help the defensive note in his voice, or the muscle that jumped in his jaw as he ground his teeth together waiting for Vin's answer.

KISS AND RIDE

"That'd be pretty hypocritical of me," Vin replied.

Luca glanced at him and saw him smirking in a way that made Luca's stomach flutter.

"Okay, then. Glad we straightened that out."

Vin snorted, then laughed, throwing his head against the seat. His laughter was contagious so soon they were both snickering as they wove through the traffic on the streets of Rome.

Luca unlocked the door of his apartment, holding it open for Vin. They wheeled their suitcases inside, and as the door closed behind them, Luca felt a sense of relief envelop him. He was home. Finally. His body was running on energy stored for emergencies, but that was running out quickly, too.

Luca waved for Vin to follow him down the corridor, giving him a quick tour of the small apartment – the living room on the left, the kitchen on the opposite side on the right, Luca's bedroom at the end of the corridor and the bathroom right next to it.

"Make yourself at home," Luca said as Vin wheeled his suitcase in the living room and set it down to unzip it. "Are you hungry?" Vin nodded. He'd gone quiet after their therapeutic laughter session in the car. Luca supposed he was running low on energy, too. "Okay, go take a shower if you want and I'll make something real quick."

With another nod Vin collected his toiletries and some clothes and headed for the bathroom.

"Spare towels are on the shelf over the radiator," Luca called after him.

While Vin was in the shower, Luca put some pasta on the stove to boil, then prepared the couch for sleeping. By the time the shower turned off, he'd set the table with two plates of fresh pasta with garlic, prawns, and cherry tomatoes.

They ate in silence, both of them too tired and overwhelmed from the hell of a day they'd had to try and muster any small talk topics. Vin didn't seem uncomfortable and Luca was glad. His wet hair was gathered on top of his head in a messy bun, and his posture was relaxed as he ate. Wearing a pair of sweats and a white t-shirt, his skin still flushed from the hot shower, Vin looked stripped of all his protective layers. He looked young and vulnerable, and Luca ached to pull him in his arms, and hold him.

Luca's eyes kept going to the tattoo on the inside of Vin's forearm. Two snakes, one white, one black, entwined together, no indication where one

KISS AND RIDE

started and the other ended. It was so beautifully done, so elegant yet poignant. In his mind, Luca saw his finger tracing the outline of the white snake, then the black, Vin's skin erupting in goosebumps under his touch.

When they were done with dinner, Luca made to clear the table, but Vin insisted he'd do it, and Luca should go take a shower, and go to bed. He didn't protest. A hot shower followed by a whole night's sleep in his own bed sounded heavenly right now.

"Hey, Luca?" Vin called after him when Luca headed for the bathroom. "Thanks," he said when Luca turned to face him. "For everything." When Luca nodded in acknowledgement, Vin quickly turned away from him and busied himself with washing the dishes.

In the morning, Luca tiptoed through the apartment, careful not to wake Vin who was snoring peacefully on the couch. The fridge was practically empty, so Luca decided to go get something to eat from the bakery across the street before waking Vin. By the time he got back, however, Vin was already awake and making coffee in the kitchen. The tempting aroma drew Luca in like a siren song. Toeing his shoes off, Luca padded to the kitchen to find Vin leaning against the table, watching the coffee maker as if willing it to hurry up. His hair was even messier than yesterday, the elastic band barely containing it on the back of his head.

"Oh, hey," Vin said with a smile, a brilliant sparkle in his blue eyes that hadn't been there the day before. "Um... I need my caffeine fix in the morning," he said, pointing at the gurgling coffee machine and looking at Luca uncertainly, as if he wasn't sure he was allowed to use it.

Luca waved his concern off, then took two plates out of the cupboard and arranged the pastries on them while Vin filled two cups with coffee, making a face when Luca said he took his black, no sugar. They didn't speak much as they ate, enjoying their food and aromatic coffees, and it felt comfortable. Luca didn't feel pressured into making small talk, and judging by Vin's relaxed posture he felt at ease, too.

When the last of the pastries were polished off the plate, they made their way to the living room, clutching their steaming mugs. Vin had folded the bedding into a neat pile on the armchair so the sofa was free to sit on.

"So? What Italian Christmas traditions are you going to expose me to today?" Vin asked, hiding his

KISS AND RIDE

grin as he took a sip of coffee. His dimples gave him away, though.

"Well, for starters, we're going shopping."

Vin didn't protest. He even seemed excited about it, getting dressed in record time in black skinny jeans slashed at the knees, a soft navy sweater, and a casual tailored jacket.

"It's not too cold outside, right?" He asked, bending down to tie his Converse.

"No, it's much like yesterday."

Vin nodded, but grabbed his scarf from the coat hanger, and after a little hesitation, fished a grey beanie from the pocket of his hanging coat. He put it on, trying to tuck all his hair underneath, and only partially succeeding, some of his curls rebelliously escaping under the hat.

Luca watched him, warm affection erupting from his heart and spreading through his body. Vin smiled at him, a little shyly, then shoved his hands in the pockets of his jeans.

"Ready when you are," he said, jerking his chin towards the door behind Luca.

Vin quickly discovered that Luca shopped much like he drove – fast, furious, and with the great determination to be as efficient as possible. Shops closed early on Christmas Eve so Vin supposed that was the reason they were in a hurry, but damn – he wanted to take his time and browse all the wonderful stores without having to jog after Luca, who was throwing things in the shopping cart like a maniac.

They went to the supermarket round the corner from Luca's apartment first. It was small and, at first glance, not much different from the independent supermarket on Vin's street in New York. The fresh fruit and vegetables were arranged neatly in colorful piles that caught Vin's eye immediately. Luca stormed through them, picking the things they'd need, and moving on further inside the store. Vin wanted to linger, touch the textures, inhale the alluring scents, remember the vivid colors. With a sigh, he followed Luca who was frowning at the slim selection of fish at the counter. Glaring at the fish, then at the counter attendant in turn, was probably the longest he'd stayed in one place ever since they'd left the apartment. Vin leaned against the counter, a smile curving his lips as he watched Luca argue with the poor fish monger.

Luca hadn't bothered with styling his hair this morning, and Vin was glad. He'd looked gorgeous yesterday, with his slicked back hair and impeccable suit, but now? Now he looked good enough to lick all over. His short hair was free to do whatever it wanted,

KISS AND RIDE

falling in soft waves in his eyes, or sticking out when Luca impatiently tried to smooth it back; his blue jeans hugged his ass in a way that made Vin's hands itch with temptation; his neatly trimmed beard, leather jacket and classic black boots completed the casual, yet sexy-as-fuck, look.

Finally satisfied with a couple of whole fish the guy managed to produce from somewhere at the back, Luca moved on to the meat counter, choosing a piece of lamb, some sausages, and a selection of cold cuts. Vin was getting bored with following Luca and looking at stuff he didn't even know what to do with. He sincerely hoped that Luca's cooking abilities would manage to turn all these ingredients into something edible. If he was counting on Vin's help he'd be rather disappointed. Vin usually had to google anything more complicated than frying eggs and steaming ramen.

When they moved to the next section of the store, browsing the shelves of pasta, canned tomatoes, and the huge selection of olive oils and balsamic vinegars, something caught Vin's eye.

"Can we get this?" He asked, holding a packed of penis-shaped pasta, and barely containing the giggle that was threatening to erupt.

"We're not having penis pasta on Christmas," Luca threw over his shoulder, but Vin could hear the smile in his voice.

"How about the day after?"

Luca shook his head in resignation when Vin threw the packet in the cart and grinned at him.

"I can't believe you can actually buy penis pasta in a regular supermarket," he said as they continued down the aisle, Luca picking stuff off the shelves and adding it to the ever growing pile of groceries in the cart.

"This is Italy. We're not prudes," he said with a wink.

They dropped off the dozen shopping bags at Luca's place before venturing out again to try and find a last minute Christmas tree and decorations. Watching Luca, his eyes twinkling every time he saw a decoration he liked or a silly little Christmas knick-knack that he had no space for in his apartment, Vin realized Luca was a huge fan of everything Christmas. A feeling of tenderness clutched at his heart every time Luca smiled with unguarded joy like a kid about to unwrap his presents.

Vin wanted to get Luca something for Christmas, and he managed to do so while Luca was engrossed in a detailed nativity scene on a shop window. They took pictures of nearly everything, numerous selfies wearing Santa hats, deer antlers, or huge, fluffy garlands tied around their necks like scarves. Looking at the pictures, Vin had to remind himself he'd only met Luca yesterday. They seemed so comfortable around each other, their body language reminding him of a couple of close friends.

Or lovers.

Vin couldn't deny he found Luca incredibly attractive, and if faced with the opportunity to do something about it he wouldn't be able to resist. And why should he? They were both single, consenting adults, their life paths intertwining for a fleeting moment in time before going their separate ways again. What was the harm in a little pleasure, a little comfort, no strings attached?

God knew Vin would appreciate the distraction. He hadn't thought about the reason he was in Rome all day, appreciating Luca's efforts to make the holidays fun and homey for both of them, and distract him from the real world for a while.

Vin needed that. He needed to take a few steps back and allow himself to let go of all the anger and hurt he'd been holding on to for far too long.

"D'you think it's too big?" Luca asked, startling Vin out of his thoughts.

"Size doesn't matter, it's how you use it," Vin said with a smirk.

Luca rolled his eyes at him and, palming to back of his neck, turned Vin's head towards a six-feet-tall, bushy Christmas tree.

It was definitely too big. But Luca was looking at it as if it was the Holy Grail and they were in a Dan Brown novel, and Vin knew they were getting that tree.

"How are we going to lug it back to your place?" In his mind, he could already see them dragging the monster tree all over the cobblestoned streets of Rome, huffing and puffing as they had to go up yet another hill, all the while carrying the shopping bags they'd already filled with Christmas decorations.

But Luca already had his phone out, furiously texting someone.

"My friend Marco will come and pick us up in ten minutes," he said with a triumphant smile. "He has a pick-up truck and we can load it on it."

"A pick-up truck?" Vin asked, raising an eyebrow. The streets of Rome were tiny, some barely big enough for Luca's Fiat, let alone a truck. He tried to remember seeing anything bigger than a Mini all day, and came up with nothing.

"Yeah, he's in a band and needs it to transport their gear around."

As promised, Marco came a few minutes later, all swagger and attitude, shaking Vin's hand with a flirty wink when Luca introduced them. He was around Vin's height, and very slim, and Vin doubted he'd be of much help with loading the tree on the bed of his truck. But Marco surprised him. He picked up the tree and with no help from either Luca or Vin, secured it on the truck, fast and efficient, no movement wasted. Same thing happened when they parked in front of Luca's apartment. In under a minute, Marco had the tree down on the pavement and was climbing back into his truck, mumbling something about his mother shouting at him if he was late for Christmas dinner.

KISS AND RIDE

"He is... um..." Vin began when Marco sped off, feeling like he should make a comment about Luca's friend, even if he'd burst in and out of their day like a tornado.

Luca laughed, but there was soft affection in his eyes. "Yeah. He is."

He passed Vin the shopping bags he was carrying and grabbed the tree, taking it inside his building. The ancient elevator seemed to be big enough to fit only the tree, so Luca had the idea to stuff it inside, press the button for the third floor, then race up the stairs to meet it on his floor. Vin was laughing too hard to be able to climb the stairs fast enough to catch the elevator, especially carrying all the shopping bags. When he made it to the second floor he heard Luca's colorful curses and the mechanical whirl of the elevator moving again.

"There was nobody downstairs a moment ago!" Luca cried in outrage when Vin finally joined him on the third floor.

"I saw an old lady carrying a Pomeranian walk in when I started up the stairs," Vin said, panting, dropping the bags on the floor unceremoniously. "And by the way, I could have stayed downstairs and sent the elevator up *after* you made it to the third floor." Luca stared at Vin with wide eyes – obviously that thought hadn't even occurred to him. "Just saying."

"Why is there a Christmas tree in the elevator?" A faint female voice carried up the several flights of stairs, followed by a dog barking.

"Sorry, Signora Mortelli," Luca shouted, leaning over the banister. "The tree is mine. Long story. Could you please send it to the third floor and I'll unload it as fast as I can?"

"Luca Romano, is that you?"

"Yes, Signora Mortelli." He lowered his voice and looked at Vin over his shoulder. "Why isn't she pressing the fucking button?"

"I don't know, man. This whole thing is too ridiculous to try and make any sense of it."

Luca stared at Vin as if he couldn't quite grasp what Vin's problem was.

"When did you come back, *caro*?" Signora Mortelli's voice carried up the three flights of stairs.

"Yesterday." Luca huffed in exasperation, taking his keys out of his pocket and tossing them to Vin. "This can take a while." Vin grinned at him as he caught the keys.

"Are you spending Christmas alone again this year?" The old lady yelled.

"Signora Mortelli, please just press the button and send the tree back up, *please*," Luca called down the stairs, resting his head against the wooden banister.

Vin unlocked the door, transferred the shopping bags to the floor inside the apartment, and leaned against the door frame, curious to see how this would

KISS AND RIDE

unfold. A sound came from downstairs, then some banging, the dog barking, and finally the elevator started moving again.

"Thank fuck," Luca muttered, straightening to meet the elevator.

When it arrived at the third floor, Luca cursed under his breath before schooling his features into a polite smile and pulling the door open.

"Signora Morelli. How did you fit in here?"

The old lady waved him off, exiting the elevator gracefully, petting her dog on the head. She was a tiny woman, no more than four feet tall, dressed in an elegant long dress, a wool coat over it, and a yellow scarf around her neck. Her dark eyes were kind as she spoke to Luca, transferring her affections from the tiny dog to him.

"When are you going to get a boyfriend, *caro*? You can't spend every Christmas alone. We, humans, are not meant to be alone. You should come over tonight, meet my grandson." She leaned closer, patting Luca on the shoulder. "He's gay, too. And very handsome."

"I know, Signora Morelli. You've told me that a few times already," Luca said, taking a step around her to get the tree out of the elevator. "Thank you for the invitation, I really appreciate it, but I already have plans."

"And who's this young man?" Signora Morelli's eyes settled on Vin when Luca stepped out of the way.

She gave him a wide smile and advanced on him, ignoring any sense of personal space.

"Hello, Signora Morelli, I'm Vincent Alesi, pleasure to meet you," Vin said, in a polite voice as he extended his hand for a handshake. Signora Morelli ignored it and pulled him in for a hug, kissing both his cheeks, and nearly squashing her fragile dog between them. It didn't seem to mind, craning its neck and licking Vin on the chin.

"Look at you, so handsome," Signora Morelli cooed when she let him go. Vin wanted to take a step back but didn't want to seem rude. Another thing he hadn't inherited from his Italian parents – the complete lack of respect for personal space. "It was about time Luca got himself a boyfriend! That boy's been running himself ragged, always working, always busy. He needs someone to come home to, you know?" Signora Morelli shook her head, her kind eyes growing serious. "And what his parents did to him? *Oddio*, they should be ashamed of themselves!"

"Signora Morelli," Luca said with an audible sigh. "Please. Let's not do this on Christmas?" He inclined his head for Vin to get inside the apartment and managed to drag the tree past Signora Morelli and the threshold.

Vin heard them as they wished each other happy Christmas, and she finally departed. Luca closed the door, locked it, and slumped against it in relief.

KISS AND RIDE

"I don't want to talk about it. Any of it," he said. Vin raised his hands in a placating gesture, but his smile grew wider. "Let's just get this thing set up so that we can finally have a drink, eh?"

They set up the tree in one corner of the living room, the fresh pine scent filling the whole apartment. Luca insisted on making them a drink and putting the dinner in the oven before decorating the tree and the rest of the house.

Watching Luca in the kitchen was fascinating. He moved with grace and purpose, his elegant, swift movements turning the pile of ingredients into a delicious meal.

"You like to cook?" Vin asked, as he put the rest of the groceries away in the fridge.

"Yes. It's always been a passion of mine."

Luca set a chopping board and a bowl full of vegetables on the table, and asked Vin to chop them while he prepared the fish. Vin knew Italians didn't eat meat on Christmas Eve so their dinner was mainly roasted vegetables, fish, and seafood pasta.

"I want to open my own restaurant one day," Luca said, his tone laced with melancholy. "My grandfather used to run a restaurant back in Sicily. I spent every summer there before he died, helping with the cooking as much as I could, or filling in for any of the waiters." Luca placed the seasoned fish in a baking dish, covered it with foil, and put it in the oven. Walking over to the table, he pulled the chair across from Vin, sat down, and simply watched him for a while, his eyes tracking Vin's movements as he chopped.

"You're originally from Sicily?" Vin asked, when Luca didn't continue. A need to get to know this beautiful man curled and settled in his chest, and he rubbed at the spot, willing the uncomfortable feeling away.

"No, my family is from Naples. I think I was about seven when my granddad bought a house with a big chunk of land in Cefalù – a village close to Palermo. He opened the restaurant shortly after." The melancholy was back in Luca's voice, but there was something else. Pain? Disappointment? Vin couldn't say.

Abruptly, Luca stood up and brought out another baking dish, piling the vegetables Vin had cut in it.

"What happened?" Vin didn't want to pry but he hated the shadows that had suddenly appeared in Luca's eyes. Bits and pieces came back to him, Luca saying he was estranged from his family, Signora Morelli's words about what his parents did to him, the sadness in Luca's voice when he'd told him he didn't want to spend Christmas alone.

"Granddad died and Grandma couldn't deal with the restaurant alone, so she closed it down. Refused to sell it, though. She lived in the huge house till the day she died."

"Couldn't your parents help?"

Luca shrugged. "They could but they didn't want to." He brought the seasoning to the table and mixed it with some oil, then poured it over the vegetables, covering the dish with foil before it joined the fish in the oven. "Grandma could be very stubborn, but she was the only person who's ever loved me and accepted me for who I was. Mom may be her daughter but they couldn't be more different."

The shadows in Luca's warm brown eyes turned stormy as he pressed his lips into a thin, pale line.

"Your parents don't like that you're gay?" Vin asked, his heart sinking as he realized where the story was going.

"That's quite the understatement." Luca busied himself with cleaning the table and putting stuff away as he talked. "When I came out to them they told me they never wanted to see me again. So I left and we haven't spoken in six years."

Vin winced. His heart ached in sympathy. He knew how it felt to be rejected by a parent, even if the circumstances were different.

"And then, two years ago, Grandma died and left me the house in Cefalù. Mom and Dad lost their shit. They'd been contesting the will ever since, bleeding me dry with lawyer fees and court bills."

Luca looked around and, when he saw there was nothing left to do, leaned against the counter with a resigned sigh. He folded his arms and met Vin's eyes.

"I'm sorry for unloading on you. It's Christmas Eve, we should be thankful for what we've got, not resentful of the things standing in our way."

Vin stood up and made his way over to Luca, stopping right in front of him. He wanted to touch him so badly, run his fingers in that messy, short hair, feel Luca's skin under his palms. Offer him the same sort of strength and comfort Luca had offered him yesterday when Vin'd fallen apart.

"You saw me badmouth my dead father in front of a church full of people, then ugly cry and nearly throw up when my aunt showed up. You have some catching up to do in the family drama department."

Luca chuckled, his shoulders relaxing. "How about no more family drama? At least for tonight? Let's make some drinks, put on some music and decorate." Luca's smile widened and the storm in his eyes cleared.

Vin liked that idea. He helped Luca make *Bombardino all'uovo*, a traditional Italian drink made of eggnog and rum. In winter, it was served heated up with a dollop of whipped cream on top. It was sweet and delicious, and very Christmassy. Luca toasted Vin with his glass, licking whipped cream from the top of his lips after he drank. Vin's eyes followed Luca's tongue as it sneaked out, wetting his lips, the moisture glistening as he smirked. Vin swallowed hard, embarrassed to have been caught staring, and looked away.

KISS AND RIDE

Back in the living room, Luca put on some music while Vin emptied the shopping bags full of decorations on the table. They danced as they hung glittering balls, snowflakes, and stars on the tree, and laughed when they messed up the lyrics of every popular song. The grin seemed permanently glued to Luca's face, and Vin loved it. It was so carefree, so relaxed and genuine that he decided he'd do anything to keep it there.

When Jon Bon Jovi's 'Please Come Home For Christmas' came on, Luca wrapped a garland around Vin's neck and pulled him closer, circling an arm around his waist. They danced, humming to the music, and it felt so good. Vin's brain was empty of anything but the feel of Luca's arms around him, the subtle shift in his body as he moved. Laying his head on Luca's shoulder, Vin pressed closer and let go of everything. He was here, in this perfect moment, and nothing else mattered.

When the song ended Luca dipped Vin down, then pulled him up and twirled him around as a grand finale. Vin laughed, losing his balance, but Luca caught him before he could fall. Faces a mere inch apart, Vin lowered his gaze to Luca's mouth, the desire to taste those luscious lips rushing through him, making him lightheaded.

When he raised his eyes back to Luca's, he wasn't smiling anymore. All humor had evaporated from his dark eyes, and what remained was the primal spark of desire that shot through Vin, making his knees go weak.

The oven timer's shrill ring broke the spell, and they pulled apart, heat rushing to Vin's cheeks. Luca didn't notice – he hurried to the kitchen to take care of their dinner.

"Fuck," Vin murmured, falling down on the couch. Rubbing his hands over his face, Vin tried to calm his erratic heartbeat and make sense of what was happening, but failing miserably. Images of Luca's lips, his smile, the sexy twinkle in his eyes kept going on a loop in his mind, pushing everything else out.

Vin leaned back, focusing on the soft glow of the colorful Christmas lights, falling over the tree like a shimmering curtain. The music kept playing softly and he could hear Luca walking around in the kitchen, opening and closing cupboards, silverware and plates clacking.

He couldn't remember when was the last time he'd felt so peaceful during the holidays. Probably when he was a kid, his mother pottering around their apartment, trying to cook traditional Christmas dinner and make the day special for Vin, even if she was a terrible cook. His mother – his beautiful, vibrant, talented mother – who'd done her best to fill the huge gap Antonio Alesi had left in Vin's life.

Vin felt his eyes prickle as he thought about his mom. He still missed her every single day, but the pain wasn't as sharp as it had once been. It felt more like a

KISS AND RIDE

chronic, dull pain that got especially bad at times like this.

"Vin?" Luca's voice was unexpectedly close, making Vin turn sharply towards the door. "Sorry, didn't mean to startle you." Vin waved him off but Luca seemed uncertain. He bit the inside of his cheek and looked away for a moment. "Dinner's ready. And I hope you're hungry because I've made a lot of food."

Vin grinned at him, the warm feeling he'd come to associate with Luca spreading like balm over his nostalgic thoughts, soothing them. Quieting them.

His mouth watered the moment the kitchen door opened, the fragrant aromas dulling all his other senses. The small table couldn't quite hold all the dishes filled with steaming hot food, so Luca had placed some on the counters. He pointed at each of them, explaining what they were and encouraging Vin to try a little bit of everything.

Vin took the plate Luca offered and filled it with seafood pasta, roasted vegetables, fish, and a few bits of *pezzetti* – fried cubes of ricotta-cheese-covered broccoli, artichokes, and zucchini. Making his way back to the table, Vin noticed the delicate table cloth, the crystal wine glasses, and the big Christmas candle serving as a center piece. Its flame glowed gently, casting shadows over the plates. Luca joined him, his own plate brimming with food, and filled their glasses with red wine.

"Merry Christmas," he said, holding his glass up to clink against Vin's. "To a happy, healthy year ahead, filled with many moments worth remembering."

"Cheers!" Vin toasted Luca's glass with a smile.

The food was amazing. Every dish Vin tried surpassed the previous one, delicate flavors melting on his tongue, and nearly making him moan.

"Wow, this is really good," he said the moment his mouth was empty long enough to speak. Luca's eyes sparkled with pride and satisfaction as they met Vin's over the glow of the candle flame.

"Glad you like it," Luca said, wiping his mouth on the crisp white linen napkin and taking a sip of his wine. "I don't get much of a chance to cook a proper traditional meal these days. I wouldn't have done it today either if it weren't for you. Not much fun cooking for one, or eating alone for that matter."

Vin took a sip of his own glass, not really sure how to respond. He was glad he was here, and frankly, there wasn't any place he'd rather be right now.

"Well, I don't usually have someone cooking for me, and I'm a disaster in the kitchen, so if it weren't for your cooking super powers tonight, I'd be eating frozen pizza or – if I was feeling adventurous – an omelette. So thank you, for taking me in and feeding me." He clinked his glass against Luca's who, for a brief moment, looked horrified at the thought of eating frozen pizza on Christmas, but his features melted into a smile when Vin winked at him.

KISS AND RIDE

The wine kept flowing, the food steadily disappearing from their plates, and they never ran out of things to talk about. Luca shared a few funny stories about passengers behaving badly on fourteen hour flights that made Vin nearly snort wine through his nose. In turn, Vin told Luca about working in the gallery where his mother used to work while studying for his Masters Degree in NYU.

"Masters Degree? How old are you?" Luca asked, giving Vin a onceover.

"I'm twenty four. Graduated from college two years ago and been trying to do my Masters part-time because I need a full-time job. That's why it's taking me so fucking long. But I can finally see the light at the end of the tunnel – I should be done by this time next year."

"Why did you decide to go for it in the first place?" Luca leaned back in his chair, his wine glass dangling from his elegant fingers, his gazed focused on Vin so intensely he felt as if Luca was stripping him bare, layer by fucking layer.

"When I turned eighteen a lawyer contacted me saying he was instructed by my father to set up a bank account for me. He gave me all these documents that I couldn't really understand, all the while thinking, why didn't he get in touch with me himself? Why send a fucking lawyer?" Vin shook his head, remembering how angry he'd been with his dad, but that anger didn't seem so consuming anymore. "As I thumbed through all the information, a handwritten piece of paper fell out. It said, 'Go to school'. I hadn't seen the man since I was five years old and that was all he had to say to me." Vin mimicked Luca's posture, leaning back in his own chair. "So, I did," he added with a shrug.

"Most people would have rebelled, done the exact opposite. Taken the money and spent it on a car or whatever, just out of spite," Luca said, a smile playing on his lips.

"I've never really been a rebel," Vin said easily. "And I had actually planned on going to school anyway. I'd applied for a couple of arts programmes at NYU and got accepted, even managed to secure some financial aid. It was a relief not having to worry about money while I was in college and focus on my studies."

"Does that mean you got your dad's talent?" Luca raised an eyebrow as if in challenge.

Vin chuckled. "I kinda did. One of my professors encouraged me to continue my education, saying that I had talent only seen 'once or twice in a generation'." Vin made air quotes around the words, biting his lips as his smile widened. "But he also said talent alone is worth nothing. You need the knowledge to back it up, and hard work to let it grow and develop. Professor Duncan inspired a strong work ethic in me. Even now if I feel miserable after a long day at the gallery and want to slack off on my assignments, in my mind I see his kind eyes fill with disappointment. And for some reason, that always gives me the extra push I need."

"You mentioned your mom used to work in the gallery. Was she an artist, too?" Luca asked, unfolding his body from the chair to go get an extra helping of fish.

"Not really. But she was passionate about art and had a keen eye." Luca sat back at the table, giving Vin an encouraging smile to keep talking. "She believed in my father's art the moment she lay eyes on a painting of his. Mom essentially made him what he was, especially in America. She became his muse, his confidant, the only person always having his back."

Images of his mother's dreamy smile as she talked about his dad floated to the front of his mind, making Vin's eyes burn. Never – not even once – had his mother spoken badly of Antonio Alesi, the man who had left her to raise their child alone. When Vin was younger he always thought his mom was blinded by his dad's artistic charisma, that she couldn't possibly still love a man who packed his bags and left them both without looking back. But as he grew older he realized there had to be more to it. The idea that his father wasn't the villain he'd always made him to be popped in his head more and more often, always to be discarded aside.

"So, wait," Luca said, resting his elbows on the table, jarring Vin out of his thoughts with the excitement in his voice. "Is your mom the girl in 'The Girl and the Rain'?"

The Girl and the Rain. Antonio Alesi's most famous painting. The painting that made him a household name. The painting that had inspired a bidding war from collectors all over the world, only to leave them disappointed when he refused to sell. The painting that had hung in some of the most famous museums and art galleries in the world.

The painting that had inexplicably disappeared from any exhibition and provoked numerous speculations about its whereabouts. His dad had refused to comment, veiling the painting's fate in even more mystery.

"Yes," Vin said simply.

"Wow." Luca's eyes grew wide. "I saw that painting at *La Galleria Nazionale* years ago, thinking it was the most beautiful piece of art I'd ever seen. There was something about it that spoke to me, you know? I'm no art critic, not by a long shot, but I enjoy looking at it. And I couldn't tear my eyes off of that painting. I went to see it over a dozen times while it was exhibited there." Luca paused, his enthusiasm for the painting making his eyes twinkle and his cheeks flush. "And now, years later, I'm having Christmas dinner with the son of the girl in the painting!"

Vin laughed. "You sound like you think it's some sort of a sign."

"I do." Luca was smiling but he gaze grew sombre.

"You believe in that kinda thing?"

"I do," Luca repeated, something flickering in his eyes as if he was wondering whether he should say more. Vin inclined his head, studying him, giving him space to weigh his words. "Every new place I visit I always throw a coin in a fountain," Luca said with a wide smile.

"And make a wish?"

"*Si*. And most of the time it comes true." Luca licked his lips, an embarrassed blush appearing on his cheeks when Vin raised a doubtful eyebrow at his statement. "A month ago, walking home in the early hours of the morning, I passed by *Fontana di Trevi*. There wasn't a single person around. I love that place, but it's always so crowded with tourists you can't really enjoy it, you know?" Vin nodded. Even if he hadn't seen the fountain yet, as a New Yorker he could relate to constantly having to fight your way through a crowd of tourists, not even noticing the things they were marvelling at anymore. "So anyway," Luca waved a hand. "I was there, looking at the fountain and a strange sort of peace came over me. I'd just received a letter from my lawyer the day before saying that my parents were going to appeal the ruling in my favour, which meant even more time lost in court battles and lawyer bills. I was disappointed and hurt and angry, but standing there, looking at the beautiful architecture, I let it all go." Luca's eyes got that far away, dreamy look they sometimes got when he talked about something he was passionate about. "I took out a coin from my pocket, made a wish, and threw it in." Luca paused, looking at Vin intensely as if he was trying to convey something to him without words.

Vin swallowed thickly, unable to look away. "What did you wish for?"

He expected him to say that he wished for the court battle to be over so he could open his restaurant, or something along those lines, but what Luca said took him off guard.

"I wished for someone to spend Christmas with." Luca's voice was soft, gentle, like a caress given to a lover. "I wished for you."

His gaze on Vin was unwavering. Unapologetic. Vin felt exposed and vulnerable under the intensity of it, a warm tingling of desire uncurling in his chest.

God, he wanted this man! This beautiful, sensual, charismatic man he'd met the day before but felt like he'd known forever. This sexy, gorgeous man with the soulful dark eyes that made his heart beat faster with a single glance.

Luca cleared his throat, looking away, a thin crease between his brows. "Shall we move to the living room? Watch some TV?"

Ice cold disappointment rushed through Vin, making him sag in his chair.

"Sure."

KISS AND RIDE

They cleaned the table, loading the dishwasher, wiping the counters and storing the leftovers away, all the while Luca protesting that Vin was his guest and shouldn't be doing this. Vin ignored him, glad he could do something to help. He was distracted, though, his mind conjuring a hundred different reasons why Luca was sending him mixed signals.

In the end, he gave up and decided to just roll with it. Nothing about this trip seemed to be going according to his plans, so he might as well stop trying to make any sense of it all.

In the living room, they settled on the couch, Luca clicking a few buttons on the remote and pulling up the Netflix app. They decided on 'A Christmas Story' and settled comfortably, turning off all the lights but the ones on the Christmas tree. Too full from dinner, and tipsy from the wine, Vin started to drift off while the title credits were still rolling on the screen.

A shiver ran through him, and then Luca's hand was on his thigh.

"Are you cold?" Luca asked softly.

"A little."

Luca stood up and a few moments later a warm, fluffy blanket that smelled like him covered Vin's body.

"Thanks," Vin said, snuggling inside the comfortable softness, letting Luca's scent envelop him. Lure him. Drug him.

Luca sat back on the far end of the couch, the blanket not long enough to reach him. He probably wasn't even cold and didn't need the blanket, but Vin couldn't help but wonder – imagine – what it would feel like to have Luca's body pressed against his under the blanket. Feel the heat from his skin, his breath on his neck, his hands on his hips.

Lifting one corner of the blanket, he inclined his head, silently inviting Luca to join him. In the few seconds it took Luca to make a decision, Vin's heart stopped. He held Luca's gaze, not backing down, making sure Luca knew exactly what Vin wanted.

Luca slipped under the blanket.

With a loud exhale, Vin could breathe again.

Luca settled behind him, his chest to Vin's back, his arm under Vin's head, his breath on Vin's skin. For the life of him Vin couldn't say what the movie they were watching was about. His eyes were staring unseeingly at the TV, but his entire being was centered around Luca's presence behind him.

Unable to control the instinct – the desire – to get closer to Luca, Vin rolled his hips, pushing his ass backwards into Luca's groin. The corresponding hardness he felt there made him grin.

Maybe the signals Luca was sending him weren't so mixed after all.

Luca's arm slid around Vin's waist and he kept him there, pressed around him, not letting him move away. Vin rolled his hips again, gasping when Luca thrust forward to meet him halfway.

"Are you sure?" Luca whispered, his breath tickling the side on Vin's neck before Luca's lips touched the skin.

"Yes," Vin said breathlessly, biting his lip to curtail the urgency trying to overtake him. He wanted to take it slow, enjoy every second without being rushed. He wanted to kiss every inch of Luca's skin, get to know his body as if it was his own. He wanted to watch Luca as he fell apart in his arms, kiss the incoherent words coming out of his mouth.

Vin turned in Luca's arms to find him frowning. Luca's arm held him close, but the hesitation in his dark eyes confused Vin.

"What's wrong?" Vin asked, his lips brushing Luca's as he spoke.

"I don't want you to think I'm taking advantage of you," Luca said, pulling slightly back to peer into Vin's eyes. "That's not why I invited you to stay with me."

Vin smiled, relief washing over him. "I know that," he said, his palm coming to rest on Luca's cheek. "I want this. I want *you*."

Luca took a few more seconds to study Vin, and then he could see the moment Luca let all his restraint go. His eyes cleared, the colorful Christmas lights reflecting in them dancing merrily. His body relaxed and melted into Vin's before Luca's tongue snuck out to wet his parted lips.

And then his mouth was on Vin's, kissing him, wet open mouthed kisses that made Vin's toes curl. Kissing had always been Vin's favorite part. There was something about touching his lips to someone else's that made heat pool at the pit of his stomach at the very thought.

But kissing Luca was something else entirely.

His lips were a gentle force; a sweet, delicious storm. They made no requests. They demanded Vin's undivided attention, and dear god, they got it.

Luca parted Vin's legs with his knee, pushing him deeper into the couch as he lay on top of him. Vin buried his hands in Luca's hair, not letting him put the slightest gap between them. A strangled moan escaped him when Luca flexed his hips, grinding his hard cock into Vin's through layers of clothes. Vin was so turned on he felt he might explode under Luca's lightest touch.

Luca's kisses grew deeper, more urgent, losing any pretence of finesse or seduction. He was exploring Vin in a primal, carnal way, losing himself in the moment. Fingers in Vin's hair, Luca made a low, whimpering sound, separating their lips to place exploring kisses and soft bites along Vin's jaw. Vin loved the feel of Luca's beard. A shiver ran through him when he felt it scrape along the tender skin on his neck.

KISS AND RIDE

"What do you want?" Luca asked in a gentle whisper, leaning back to look at Vin. He didn't know what Luca saw, but his dark eyes grew impossibly darker, his teeth digging into his lower lip.

"I like... everything," Vin said, his fingers tightening into the skin of Luca's hip. "But right now I need you inside me."

Luca's eyes fluttered closed, his brows pulling down. For a moment Vin thought he'd disappointed him, that maybe Luca preferred to bottom, but when he looked at Vin again there was no mistake Luca wanted it, too.

"I'll go get the condoms and lube," Luca murmured, lowering his mouth to Vin's for a gentle, exploring kiss. It deepened, grew heated, made Vin see stars every time Luca nipped at his lip or sucked it into his mouth. Their groins kept grinding lazily against each other, the pressure building in Vin's balls.

"Go get the condoms, Luca," Vin managed to say between kisses. "Or soon we won't need them." Vin felt Luca's lips spread into a smile against his own, and then the comforting heat of Luca's body on top of his was gone.

The urgency Vin was trying so hard to rein in bubbled to the surface again. Hands shaking, he pulled his shirt over his head, dropping it to the floor. His sweats followed, but he hesitated as he hooked his thumbs in the waistband of his boxers. Maybe he should leave some packaging for Luca to unwrap himself?

Vin heard Luca's footsteps as he came closer, but he stopped by the couch instead of falling on top of Vin as he'd hoped. Lube in one hand and condoms in the other, Luca's eyes raked up and down Vin's body, his throat working as he swallowed hard.

Vin'd never been self-conscious about his body – he was a bit too thin and could use some muscles, but the thought of sweating in the gym every day repulsed him. But as Luca loomed over him, staring, cataloguing every inch of skin, every line of ink, every freckle, Vin couldn't resist the urge to squirm.

"You going to stand there all night?" Vin said, pulling on his boxers to reveal the neatly trimmed hair underneath.

"Don't you dare," Luca said with a low growl, making quick work of his clothes and kneeling between Vin's legs.

His tight briefs stood no chance in containing his impressive erection. Vin's stomach fluttered in anticipation. It'd been more than a year since he'd let anyone fuck him, and he hadn't been as well hung as Luca.

Replacing Vin's fingers with his own, Luca pulled his boxers down, slowly, his eyes glued to the movement. Vin's hard cock sprang free, flopping on his belly, a pearly drop glistening on its tip. Getting rid of the boxers entirely, Luca lowered his body on top of

KISS AND RIDE

Vin's, mouths meeting half way, hands roaming bare skin.

"Your turn," Vin murmured against Luca's lips, hooking his fingers in the elastic of his briefs.

Luca lifted his hips to help him get the briefs past his ass, and Vin left them there, his hands too busy kneading the soft flesh. With a frustrated growl, Luca leaned back on his haunches, taking his underwear off. The sight of his gorgeous hard cock made Vin's mouth water. He sat up, wrapped his arms around Luca's waist and kissed his way up his chest, sucking on his nipples, teeth scraping smooth skin.

"I want to taste you," he said, lips moving against Luca's neck.

Luca grabbed the tousled knot of hair on Vin's head, pulling him back and away from his skin.

"Later," he rasped, slanting his mouth over Vin's and toppling them back down on the couch.

"But..." Vin tried to protest, but his words got lost in a needy whimper when Luca pressed their hard cocks together, rolling his hips and making Vin forget how to speak.

"I said," Luca whispered in Vin's ear, licking the shell and nipping at the lobe. "Later."

Vin managed a small nod, his back bowing off the couch looking for more intense contact. Luca propped his body weight on his elbows on both sides of Vin's head, denying him the harder friction he craved.

"Luca..." Vin managed, the rest of his words lost in an urgent whimper.

Luca moved on top of him, hand patting the floor for the condoms he'd dropped. In his lustful haze, Vin barely registered Luca opening the packet and sheathing his cock, his attention focusing on Luca's slick fingers as he worked him open.

Willing himself to relax, Vin traced the skin on Luca's shoulder with his tongue, kissing the warm, enticing spot in the crook of his neck. The gentle pressure of Luca's fingers was driving him insane. He needed more, he needed to feel Luca inside him before he lost his mind.

"Fuck me, Luca," he said, biting on Luca's neck. "Fuck..." The rest of his words died on his tongue when he felt the head of Luca's cock breach him.

Luca panted on top of him, intently gazing in his eyes, watching for Vin's reaction as he slowly slid inside him. Vin dug his nails in Luca's skin, biting his lip through the uncomfortable stretch. Luca stilled once he was fully inside him, giving him time to adjust, but the effort of holding back was clearly written on his face.

Vin arched his back, silently urging Luca to move, his fingers probably leaving red marks on Luca's skin by now. Gently, Luca pulled back, then thrust back in, making Vin's eyes roll with pleasure.

KISS AND RIDE

"You feel so good," Luca said with a low groan, his hand sliding down to Vin's hip, bruising his flesh with the intensity of his hold.

The slow pace Luca had started was not enough for Vin, not anymore. Wrapping his legs around Luca's waist, he grabbed the back of his neck and brought his mouth down for a kiss. Luca got the hint, his movements getting faster, harder, more erratic. He clutched Vin's thigh, thrusting in and out of him with mindless urgency, his kisses getting hungrier, louder, more desperate.

Vin knew instinctively Luca was close. He was, too, but he didn't want to let go of any part of Luca to wrap his hand around his own cock. He'd never come hands free before, but he was really close now as Luca was nailing the sensitive spot inside him nearly every time.

"Fuck, right there!" Vin rasped, his voice catching on the last word.

Luca buried his face in Vin's neck, pounding into him, clutching at his thigh with one hand, the other tangled in Vin's messy hair. Closing his eyes, all Vin could feel was Luca's touch, his breath on his skin, his scent everywhere around him, his harsh pants getting more and more urgent.

Vin came without any warning, the pleasure exploding inside his body without him even touching his cock. Luca kept fucking him through it, pulling back slightly to stare at him, then cupped his cheek and kissed him. The tortured sounds he made as his own orgasm peaked were lost between them, swallowed by their kiss. His body trembled on top of Vin's, his cock pulsing inside him until Luca was entirely spent.

Their lips stayed locked for a while, the intensity of the kiss melting into a languid exploration. As Vin's heartbeat finally slowed down, he felt the sweat drying on his skin and a chill ran through him. Luca slipped out of him gently, but the move still made Vin wince.

"You okay?" Luca asked, studying Vin's face for the answer rather than expecting a reply.

"Yeah," Vin said with a smile. "More than okay."

Standing, Luca offered Vin a hand and pulled him up, wrapping an arm around him and pulling him against his chest. He made a face at the mess of hair currently tied on top of Vin's head and gently untangled the elastic band. Vin's curls fell loose around his face, making Luca smile as he raked a hand through them.

The moment felt different, in a way more intimate than the sex they'd just had. Luca was looking at him with what could only be described as affection, and Vin's heart sped up again. Nobody had ever looked at him like that; Vin didn't know how to react. His eyes stayed glued to Luca's face – he didn't want to miss a single flicker of emotion that passed behind those dark eyes.

KISS AND RIDE

"Let's go to bed, *tesoro*," Luca murmured, placing a soft kiss on Vin's parted lips.

Vin nodded, letting Luca lead him to his bedroom – to his bed – where he snuggled in Luca's waiting arms under the blanket, the distant chime of the church bells announcing the arrival of Christmas lulling him to sleep.

They slept in the next morning. They needed it, after waking several times during the night, hands exploring naked skin, mouths finding each other in the dark. Luca had never felt such bottomless desire for another person. It was like Vin had cast a spell on him and he couldn't get enough.

The bells in the basilica across the road tolled again, as they'd been doing for hours. It was Christmas, so they'd be going off even more than usual. Luca was used to it, didn't even register the sound anymore, but Vin had stirred every time the bells chimed, his warm pliant body finding another angle to curl around Luca.

"Fucking bells, man," Vin murmured, his eyes still closed, but a frown forming between his brows. "We get it, it's Christmas, now shut the hell up."

Luca laughed quietly, kissing Vin's temple and trying to smooth his wild hair back. It was an impossible task, so Luca soon gave up, tangling his fingers in it instead.

"How do you ever get any sleep?" Vin asked, then yawned, resting his cheek on Luca's chest and opening his eyes to look at him.

"I don't usually have an insatiable guy in my bed to keep me up all night, so sleep's never a problem."

Vin snuck a hand under Luca's hips and pinched his ass. Luca arched off the bed, laughing.

"I meant, the fucking church bells," he said, sternly, but the corners of his mouth soon lifted.

"When you've been hearing them since you were born you don't even register them anymore. It's all background noise to me now."

"Is it like that all across Italy?"

"Pretty much, yeah."

Vin grunted in response, closing his eyes again, his fingers tracing Luca's ribs absentmindedly.

"I'm going to need a nap later. And some ear plugs."

"It's Christmas day. All we're going to do today is eat, sleep and make out."

KISS AND RIDE

Vin's cheeks dimpled as he smiled widely, lifting his head off Luca's chest and brushing his lips against his collarbone.

"I like that a lot."

"But first," Luca said, smacking Vin's ass under the blanket. "Shower."

The much needed shower lasted a lot longer than Luca's usual five minutes. Vin took his time lathering Luca's body with soap, massaging the knots on his back under the hot water, then dropping to his knees and sucking his cock until Luca spilled in his mouth. The water was getting cold by then, and Vin pushed him out of the bath tub, not letting him return the favor, and quickly finished with his own shower. By the time he was done, he was shivering from the cold water, gratefully accepting the towel Luca wrapped around his shoulders.

For breakfast, Luca reheated the leftovers from last night, then let Vin wash the dishes while he set on preparing their Christmas dinner.

"What's your favorite pasta dish?" Luca asked Vin, who was wiping his hands on a kitchen towel and watching the coffee machine as it dripped lazily into the pot.

"Lasagna," Vin replied without hesitation. "It was the only thing my mom knew how to make." Vin smiled fondly as if a pleasant memory was floating in his mind. "Every Friday night we'd go to the Italian market a couple of blocks away and we'd buy all the ingredients. She had a sweet tooth, so we always got a dessert as well. Mrs Russo, the owner's wife, made epic tiramisu. She always put a box aside for us because it usually sold out by noon."

Luca smiled, accepting the coffee cup Vin handed him and they sat at the table.

"Then we'd go home and we'd cook together. It was always the highlight of my week." Vin's eyes became unfocused as he brought the mug to his lips. "Why do you ask?" He added distractedly, as if just now remembering Luca's original question.

"Because I'm making a pasta dish today."

Vin's eyebrows pulled down in confusion. "I thought you were making that lamb shank we bought"

"That, too."

"But it's just the two of us. Who's going to eat all that food?"

"I haven't cooked Christmas dinner in ages," Luca said, and even though he kept his tone light he saw Vin's gaze soften. "So I'm going to do it properly, and I'm going to make enough food for a small village, and we're going to eat it all."

Vin grinned, then nodded. "Fine. But I want to help."

They spent the next few hours cooking in the kitchen. Luca brought his iPod dock from the living room, and played his favorite holiday playlist. When 'Let it Snow' came on he pulled Vin into his arms and they danced in the middle of the kitchen, food preparation temporarily on pause.

Vin claimed to have no idea what he was doing, but Luca noticed he approached every task he gave him methodically and with great determination. The pasta machine, however, was his favorite. Vin spent nearly an hour rolling dough through the pasta machine, then cutting out different shapes, completely engrossed in his project. Luca watched him, and even though they didn't need that much pasta, he left him to it. In his mind, that was what Vin always looked like when he was creating something, whether it was miniature irregular pasta shapes, a painting or a sculpture carved out of stone.

When there was no more dough to roll through the machine, Vin finally looked up from his creations. The entire table was covered in layers of pasta, each and every one of them uniquely beautiful.

"Thank god I have enough space in the freezer," Luca said, folding his arms and staring at the pasta.

Vin looked uncertain for a moment, wiping his hands on the apron Luca had given him and blowing a loose strand of hair from his face. He had flour smeared on his nose and cheekbone, his blue eyes dark with creative inspiration.

Luca couldn't resist him even if he wanted to. Hooking a finger in the apron, he pulled Vin closer, kissing his soft lips, then smiling against them.

"You're so fucking sexy when you're that focused on something," he murmured, the tip of his tongue sliding out to coax Vin's lips open.

Vin hummed, wrapping his arms around Luca's neck, burying his fingers in his hair to keep him in place. Luca knew they'd both need another shower after they were done cooking. Neither of them cared if they got messy as they made out.

Luca could already picture Vin's wet skin, rivulets of water sliding down his back as Luca fucked him against the wall, then turned him around to suck him off, Vin staring down at him through hooded eyes, drops of water rolling down his stomach. Luca's cock filled and hardened, and he deepened the kiss, walking Vin backwards until his back hit something. The wall, the fridge, the fucking counter – Luca didn't care. He kept kissing him, blind and deaf for everything around him but the feel of Vin's hands in his hair, his slim body pressed against his, his keen moans and whimpers as Luca explored his mouth with his tongue.

KISS AND RIDE

"I want you." The words slipped out of Luca's mouth in a harsh breath, caught between their lips. Vin moaned eagerly, hands sliding down Luca's back, pulling him even closer, too far gone to form any actual words. "Shower," Luca managed to say, then grabbed Vin's hand and pulled him towards the bathroom.

In the shower, Luca did exactly what he'd imagined he'd do to Vin next time he had him naked and wet under the hot water. Grabbing a condom from the cabinet over the sink, Luca pulled the shower curtain closed and pinned Vin against the wall. The water was cascading over them, making their kisses wetter and more urgent as they gasped for breath.

Luca spun Vin around, pressing him against the wall, his hard cock nestled against Vin's ass. Curving his spine and pushing his ass out, Vin groaned when Luca rubbed his shaft between his ass cheeks.

"Fucking do it," Vin said, his voice hoarse and urgent, his need hitting Luca straight in the gut.

Quickly sheathing his cock, Luca pressed inside Vin, slowly, pushing steadily until he was buried inside him. He rested his forehead between Vin's shoulder blades, trying to gain some control, but his eyes landed on the spot their bodies joined and he nearly lost it right there. With a gentle roll of his hips, Luca pulled out a little, watching as his cock slid out of Vin's body. Vin trembled in his arms, impatient, eager, wanting.

Luca wanted to take his time but it wasn't going to happen. They were both too far gone for that.

Reaching in front of Vin, Luca wrapped his fingers around Vin's cock at the same time as he started thrusting in and out of him, the movement pushing Vin's shaft into his fist. Curses and desperate pleas for *harder*, *more*, *right there*, rolled out of Vin's mouth, urging Luca on. He wrapped an arm around Vin, pulling him off the wall and holding him flush against his chest, his hand on his cock speeding up as he rocked his hips faster, losing all sense of rhythm. Vin came with a hoarse cry, his cock pulsing in Luca's hand, just as Luca felt his own orgasm taking over his body.

Carefully, Vin turned in his arms and kissed him, softly, gently, taking his breath away. Luca had to pull back, it was too much, too soon. His heart was about to burst with everything he felt for Vin, and he needed to protect it.

But when he looked in Vin's eyes, deep blue under the cluster of wet lashes, Luca knew it was already too late.

KISS AND RIDE

They ate dinner in the kitchen, the music playing quietly in the background, the wine flowing, candles burning all around them. It had been Vin's idea to turn the lights off and light every candle they could find in Luca's apartment. Luca had to admit it did make the atmosphere more festive, and the room seemed different. He wasn't sure if it was the candles or the fact that Vin was there or the delicious food Luca got to cook so rarely these days, but what he was absolutely certain of was that his kitchen had never been so enticing.

Vin praised Luca's cooking, making him feel ridiculously proud while he watched Vin close his eyes in bliss as he tried the lamb for the first time. Soon, the first bottle of wine was empty and they opened another one, eating slowly, savouring every taste, and talking – all evening, they never ran out of things to talk and laugh about.

Too full to eat another bite, they took their glasses and moved to the living room. They left the lights off, carrying a few candles from the kitchen and only turning on the colorful Christmas lights on the tree. It didn't feel right to have an empty table on Christmas, so Luca brought a bowl of dried fruit and nuts, as well as the plate with the *pandoro*, and placed them on the coffee table. Vin groaned when he saw the food, but Luca could see the spark of interest in his eyes as they landed on the *pandoro*. Unable to resist the light, fluffy cake, Vin threw Luca a glare before cutting a piece for both of them. He fed Luca the first bite, then tried it himself, and refused to give Luca any more bites from his slice.

"I thought you were too full," Luca said, cutting another slice from the cake for himself.

"I was!" Vin said, mouth full of cake. "But this is so good!"

They chased down the *pandoro* with some more wine, the fruity undertones of the Merlot going perfectly with the cake.

"Oh, I nearly forgot!" Vin said, jumping to his feet and walking out of the room. He came back a moment later with a small package wrapped in green paper, a red bow on top of it. "I got you something." He handed Luca the gift, smiling shyly.

"When did you manage that?" Luca took the gift, but put it on the table, heading to his room to get Vin's gift.

"When we went shopping the other day. You were distracted by some nativity scene and I managed to buy it before you noticed." Vin sounded very proud of himself, his face lighting up when Luca came back and handed him his gift. "Sneaky," he said with a wink.

Grinning like children, they opened their gifts at the same time. Luca laughed when he saw the pair of blue socks with perfectly shaped male butts all over them, and Vin wrapped the scarf Luca had gotten him around his neck, kissing Luca on the cheek. It suited him perfectly, just as Luca'd thought it would – pale green with dark blue stripes on it, nearly the same as Vin's eyes.

"We really need to leave the bed at some point," Luca said, pulling a breathless Vin into his arms.

They'd been waking up every few hours to have sex, and Vin was both sated and exhausted. But he couldn't resist Luca's touch. It made every cell in his body come to life and hum with pleasure.

"Why?" Vin asked, resting his chin on Luca's shoulder.

Luca raked a hand through Vin's hair, smoothing it back away from his face, and studied him with dark eyes under hooded lids. A smirk played on his kiss-swollen lips as he put his arm under his head to see Vin better.

"Because I want to show you Rome. It's beautiful."

"You're beautiful," Vin said, too content to try and measure his words.

Luca's smirk widened into a full blown grin. "True," he said, squirming when Vin tickled his ribs. "But flattery is not going to get you out of this. We're going sightseeing today."

Luca made him breakfast and then resisted Vin's attempts to lure him back to bed. With a heavy sigh, Vin realized there really was no getting out of this, so he took a quick shower and got dressed.

The early morning air felt cold on Vin's cheeks, so he pulled the scarf Luca had given him closer around his neck. It wasn't anything near as cold as the harsh New York winter, but after spending a couple of days cooped up in Luca's cosy apartment Vin could definitely feel the chill.

They grabbed two cups of coffee from the bakery across the street, the hot liquid warming Vin and awakening his senses. Luca held Vin's hand as they walked leisurely up and down the cobble-stone streets, and Vin didn't protest. He wasn't into PDAs per se, but Luca's hand felt good in his and he didn't want to let go. He wouldn't think twice about it if they were in New York, but Italy was a conservative country when it came to homosexuality. Even in a cosmopolitan, diverse city such as Rome Vin wondered if they'd get any strange looks.

Luca didn't seem to care. He held Vin's hand, pulled him in for a hug every once in a while, smiled at him in a way that was plainly obvious they weren't just friends, and even kissed him when they took a selfie in

KISS AND RIDE

front of the Colosseum, the humongous Christmas tree right in front of it serving as a festive backdrop.

The Colosseum was as grandiose as Vin had imagined it to be. Inside, Vin felt the air shift, and if he closed his eyes he could hear the roar of the crowds. Fascinated, he touched the stone remains as he passed by them, letting them tell him their story. The Colosseum buzzed under his fingertips, like an electric current; the fights, the struggles, the cruelty, the smell of blood and sweat and misery – they all blended in Vin's mind, creating a beautiful, tragic picture.

Vin swayed on his feet, his mind so engrossed in the intense feelings this building was evoking in him that he felt dizzy. Luca grabbed for his arm, steadying him, concerned dark eyes meeting his.

"You okay?"

"Yeah. It's just this place. It's consuming."

Luca studied him for a few moments, but didn't say anything else. As if sensing Vin's mind was working on another wavelength right now, Luca gave him space. He was always within an arm's reach, though, ready to prop Vin back up if he lost his footing.

Outside, Vin asked if they could sit down for a cup of coffee somewhere. Luca took him to a small coffee shop tucked away in a side street, tiny round tables clustered on the sidewalk. The sun was shining, making the day even more pleasant, and they decided to sit outside to enjoy their drinks.

As soon as Vin sat down, he reached for the stack of napkins on the table – nice, thick ones, thankfully – pulled out a pen from his jacket pocket, and started drawing. He needed to get the buzzing out of him, and if he had to do it on a paper napkin with a crappy pen then so be it. It was like a pent up frustration, or too much emotion, or caged anger that needed to be released. And until it was, Vin was blind to anything else.

By the time he was done, his coffee was getting cold, and he hadn't even noticed when the waiter had brought it. In a daze, Vin looked around, noticing the untouched cup in front of him, and Luca, who was playing on his phone, two empty cups in front of him.

"How long have we been here?" Vin asked, as the fog started to clear in his mind.

"About an hour," Luca said, looking up from his phone. He smiled at Vin, inclining his head as he watched him.

Vin didn't know what Luca saw, but his penetrating gaze made him squirm. He always got the feeling Luca was seeing more than Vin was willing to show.

"Sorry, I didn't mean to space out, but sometimes it hits me, you know? And I need to get it out and I'm completely useless until I do."

Luca waved him off, resting his elbows in the table and staring at Vin intently, as if seeing him for the first time.

KISS AND RIDE

"So, did you? Get it out?"

Vin shrugged. "Some of it, yeah. But my guess is I'll have a lot of inspiration to work with when I get back home."

Luca winced, but quickly recovered. "Glad to hear it. Told you Rome is beautiful." He winked at Vin, then signalled for the waiter to bring them the check.

They spent the rest of the day walking around, Vin taking a thousand pictures on his phone of anything that remotely caught his interest. Rome was simply amazing, so much history in every corner. Vin had a degree in Fine Arts so he knew a lot about Roman culture and art. He could name the artist behind every famous sculpture and the architect behind a historic building; he knew what was built when and by whom, when it was destroyed, and who renovated it; he could write a thesis on the influence and importance of Roman culture.

But experiencing Rome in person was nothing like reading about it on paper.

Vin was overwhelmed. Not just by Rome's power over him, but by discovering little things he knew nothing about, and thinking – wondering – if his dad had walked these same streets, fascinated and inspired by everything he was seeing.

As if sensing Vin's growing melancholy, Luca took him to an ice-cream place that had one hundred and fifty flavors of *gelato*, and was conveniently located close to the Pantheon. A little pit stop that did wonders for relaxing Vin's mind. Huge ice-cream cones in hand, they continued on their exploration of the city. When the sun started to set in the late afternoon, and the festive lights flickered to life, Luca took Vin to the famous Spanish steps. Despite the December chill, lots of people were sitting on the steps, some taking selfies, others talking to their friends or reading a book or playing on their phones. A giant, lavishly decorated Christmas tree stood on top of the steps, as if keeping watch on everyone, making sure they knew what time of the year it was and acted accordingly.

"I think it's time," Luca said, standing up from where they were sitting on top of the steps and glancing at his watch.

"For what?" Vin asked, standing up, too, and hopping down the steps after Luca.

"*Fontana di Trevi,* the last stop of our sightseeing tour today." Luca reached for Vin's hand as the descended the steps and they headed for the most famous fountain in the world.

"But what did you mean, it's time?"

"I wanted you to see it at night, when it's dark and the lights are on." Luca kept walking briskly, and Vin nearly had to run to keep up with him. "I'll take you to see it during the day, too, if you want, but I wanted your first impression to be after sunset."

Piazza di Trevi, where the fountain was situated, was shockingly small. Despite the late hour, the fact that it was a day after Christmas, and the chill in the air, it was crowded. Luca swiftly made his way through the crowd, pulling Vin behind him. Spotting an open space between a group of people right in front of the fountain, Luca hurried that way, shuffling them both between the cluster of bodies.

Vin was too engrossed in the fountain to feel uncomfortable as people jostled him, stepped on his feet and talked loudly in different languages. *Fontana di Trevi* was magnificent. Much bigger than Vin had expected; *Palazzo Poli* right behind it giving the impression of even larger grandeur. Water fell from every part of the big sculpture, making a loud, rhythmic sound that seemed to create its own melody. Lights in every color lit up the fountain, and the water, creating a magical illusion.

"That's Neptune," Luca said in Vin's ear, wrapping his arms around him from behind. Vin rested his head on Luca's chest, relaxing in his arms, surrendering to Luca's melodic voice. His gaze landed on the statue of a muscular, bearded man standing in a large shell chariot, wearing nothing but a loose robe around his hips – the focal point of the fountain. He looked every bit the Roman God of the sea, commanding everyone's attention while the rest of the statues orbited around him, waiting for his command. "See the two sea horses pulling his chariot?" Vin nodded, his eyes landing on the stone carved creatures in front of him. "See how one is docile, ready for his master's command, and the other is restless, barely held by the god's servant?" Vin nodded again, the crowds around them disappearing as his mind drifted into itself, creating and imagining, expanding, on its own accord. "The legend says they represent the vile mood swings of the sea. One moment it's smooth, crystal waters, luring you in, promising you safety and control, and the next it swallows you whole as if you're nothing more than a drop of water."

A shudder ran through Vin. He could see it, the statues coming to life, the wild horses galloping, Neptune's eyes blazing with power.

Luca kept talking, telling Vin what the rest of the statues represented, small details and superstitions Vin hadn't heard before. He could name the architect of the fountain, the year it was built, and its original purpose. But listening to Luca talk smoothly in his ear transported him to another reality altogether where Vin could feel the beauty – the magic – of the fountain.

Luca's arms tightened around him, anchoring him to the present. Vin floated back, the noise of the water and people chatter around them abusing his senses.

Looking around he saw people throwing coins in the water, closing their eyes and making wishes. Luca followed Vin's gaze, then asked,

"Would you like to throw a coin in?"

Vin shook his head. "I have nothing to wish for."

KISS AND RIDE

Luca stilled behind him, the moment of silence between them stretching for a long time. Vin didn't elaborate, didn't laugh it off, didn't pretend the words weren't as sad as they sounded.

"Actually," Luca finally said, leaning to place a soft kiss on Vin's neck. "Everyone's doing it wrong. Only Romans can make a wish. According to local superstition, if you're a foreigner, you have to throw the coin over your right shoulder. More than that, you don't get to make a wish."

"No?" Vin asked, turning in Luca's arm to face him. "What do you do then?"

"If you throw a single coin in, you're bound to return to Rome. Two coins and you'll find new love. Three coins and you'll get married soon."

Vin laughed, inclining his head to study Luca. "Is that true?"

"Anything you believe in is true."

Later, snuggled on the couch watching 'Love Actually', his head in Luca's lap, Vin couldn't concentrate on what was happening on the screen. His mind kept buzzing, all the feelings and emotions from the last few days not letting him relax. Feeling confused and helpless, Vin had no idea what to do. He was going home in a few days, and then what? Pretend like this trip never happened? Pretend like his father hadn't died? Pretend like he didn't have a million questions he wanted answers to?

His eyes widened when an idea popped into his head. An idea he hadn't even considered before because he thought he would never be ready.

"I need to call Maria, my aunt. I need to see her," he said, abruptly sitting up and startling Luca. Vin was ready to ask all his questions, but he wasn't sure he could face the answers on his own. "Will you come with me?"

Maria lived in Trastevere – a trendy neighbourhood in Rome that was about a forty minute walk from Luca's apartment. He offered to drive them there, but Vin shook his head, wrapping the scarf Luca had given him

KISS AND RIDE

around his neck and walking out of the front door without a word. He'd been like this ever since he'd called Maria last night and arranged for them to meet. It broke Luca's heart to see the haunted look in Vin's eyes. It was even worse than the melancholy stare he'd adopted after their sightseeing tour yesterday.

So, they walked. Luca thought they could both use the fresh air, and Vin would have time to clear his head and at least try and keep it together when they got to Maria's place. And if he didn't... If he didn't Luca would be there, quietly supporting him.

When they got to Maria's building, Vin hesitated before pressing the button on the buzzer. Meeting Luca's eyes he bit his lip, the uncertainty in his blue gaze startling. Luca didn't nod or shake his head, or influence his decision in any way. It was Vin's choice to make. If he'd changed his mind and wanted to leave, they'd leave.

Closing his eyes for a moment, Vin took a deep breath and pressed the button.

The door buzzed a few seconds later, letting them in. Maria was waiting for them when they took the stairs to the second floor. She looked as put together as she'd been at the memorial service in a crisp green sleeveless dress, a pashmina around her shoulders, and her dark hair in a perfectly styled ponytail. Her blue eyes sparkled as she smiled at them, hugging Vin as if it was the most natural thing in the world. Luca could see the stiff curve of his spine as he accepted the hug but didn't reciprocate. Releasing him, Maria hugged Luca in turn and kissed him on both cheeks before ushering them in.

They sat in her living room, Vin on one end of the sofa leaving enough space for Luca to join him, and Maria in the armchair opposite. She offered them drinks, but they both declined. Vin sat awkwardly, hands in his lap, rarely meeting Maria's eyes. Her own composure seemed shaken when the silence stretched, nobody daring to break it.

Clearing her throat, Maria said, "I'm really glad you decided to call, Vincent. Truthfully, I had my doubts you ever would."

Vin didn't really acknowledge her words. Instead, he lifted his chin defiantly, studying his aunt for a long moment before speaking.

"Why didn't he want me?" He asked, his gaze unwavering.

To her credit, Maria didn't flinch. She seemed to measure her words for a while, and then she said,

"Your father was a complicated man, Vincent."

Vin snorted, shaking his head. "If you're going to feed me some bullshit lines about what a great man Antonio Alesi was, save it. I've already googled it."

Maria's lips thinned, but she didn't otherwise comment. Luca had a feeling she was used to dealing with temperamental men like Vin, and knew exactly how to handle him.

KISS AND RIDE

"Tell me, Vincent, did you want for anything during your childhood?"

Vin's brows drew down in confusion. "No, I guess I didn't. Mom had a good job at the gallery and we never had any issues with money."

Maria inclined her head. "You think your mother's job at the gallery provided for all the bills, rent, your weekly art tutor? How much do you think she made?"

Vin looked lost for a moment, glancing at Luca, silently asking for support. Luca placed a hand on his knee and squeezed.

"What are you trying to say?"

"I'm trying to say that your father may not have been there in person but you can be sure he provided for his family." Vin went awfully still under Luca's hand, like a coiled snake ready to pounce.

"So, what? I'm supposed to be thankful he paid child support after he ran off?" Vin said with a sneer.

"I'm not telling you how you're supposed to feel, Vincent. I'm only giving you the facts."

"What was his excuse for refusing to take me in when Mom died?" Vin said, his anger melting away as suddenly as it had appeared, his lower lip trembling.

Maria's eyes softened and she leaned forward in the armchair, holding Vin's gaze for a long moment.

"Were you placed in a good family, Vincent?"

Her question threw Vin off again. "Yes," was all he said, his frown deepening.

"Your father made sure of that."

"But," Vin stammered, rubbing his neck with a trembling hand. "How?"

"Anything is possible when you know the right people, have good lawyers and have enough money to burn."

"I don't get it," Vin said after taking a moment to absorb the new information. "Why would he go through all this trouble? He left us! Mom never got over him, never even considered another relationship. And I spent my entire childhood idolizing him, and then slowly beginning to hate him for what he'd done to us." Vin paused, running a hand through his hair, trying to collect himself. "You're trying to tell me he cared about us, but it doesn't make any sense to me. He never called me, or wrote to me, or expressed any interest in me whatsoever. Who does that? You're trying to justify his actions by saying he sent us money and made sure we were taken care of, but it takes more than fucking money to take care of someone. From where I'm standing it seems more like he was satisfying his control issues, pulling the strings on our lives, making sure we played by his rules." Pink blotches appeared on Vin's cheeks as his words got more and more heated. Maria held his gaze, unflinching, patiently waiting for him to finish.

"Are you done?" She asked when Vin rubbed a hand over his face and fell quiet.

"He could have just *stayed*," he whispered.

KISS AND RIDE

"That's the one thing he couldn't do, Vincent."

"Why not?"

Maria leaned back in the armchair with a heavy sigh. Her composure seemed to crumple around the edges as she spoke.

"Antonio was diagnosed with manic depression when he was fifteen." Vin's eyes narrowed as he studied Maria, trying to make sense of her words. "He was put on medication, but he hated it and refused to take it. Our parents forced it on him, and it did nothing but make things worse. He ran away soon after and we didn't hear from him for three years."

"But he was a minor! Didn't your parents call the police?" Vin asked.

"They did, of course. But he was nowhere to be found." Maria looked away, her eyes growing unfocused in a way Vin's often did when he was reminiscing about something. Luca watched him as his mouth opened and closed a few times, obviously burning with questions, but he stayed silent. "He resurfaced when he turned eighteen and nobody could force him to go back to our parents' house. He got in touch with me, but made it clear he had no intention of ever contacting them. I resented my parents for chasing my brother away, and he knew it. Long story short, I packed my bags and followed him here, in Rome, and never looked back."

"Where was he born?" Vin asked in a small voice, and Luca's heart squeezed painfully in his chest.

"Lugo. It's a small town near Bologna." Vin absorbed the information and with a little nod prompted Maria to continue. "His condition got worse as time passed. There were days he couldn't function on his own, and yet he still refused to take any medication. It made him docile, he said. It interrupted the creative flow." Maria met Vin's eyes, instinctively knowing she'd touched on a raw nerve.

Vin'd said at his father's memorial service that Antonio Alesi didn't care about anything but his art, and it seemed like he'd been right.

"Antonio could live with the suffocating depression, the vile mood swings, the mad adrenalin rush that hit him when he least expected it, but he couldn't live without creating. Take that away from him and you might just as well put a bullet in his head. Our parents never got that, but I did. Your mother did, too."

Vin bristled at the mention of his mother, but Maria smiled at him, cutting off any snarky remark he might make.

"I've never met Valentina in person, unfortunately, but we often talked on the phone. She was a remarkable woman. I'm so sorry for your loss, Vincent."

Vin nodded his thanks, then asked, "If she knew... understood my dad's illness, then why did he leave? Couldn't they work through it? They must have made it work for a while – I never knew about it and certainly never saw anything unusual in his behaviour."

KISS AND RIDE

"You were a child, Vincent, a baby. How could you have seen?" Maria shook her head, folding her hands in her lap. "Valentina couldn't leave you alone with him, even for a few hours. He'd forget you existed when he got into one of his moods or when he was working on something. She'd call me, crying, exhausted for having to take care of two people, instead of just you. Love was never a problem for them. They were soulmates, of that I'm sure. But Antonio wasn't easy to live with. He could be destructive, sometimes even dangerous. They'd fight about his refusal to get help more and more often, until it took its toll on them."

Vin's blue eyes seemed nearly colorless in the light streaming through the curtains. Standing up, he took the few steps to the window, leaned on the frame and stared unseeingly outside. Luca knew it was a lot to take in, that Vin needed some space to think before he asked any more questions. Maria seemed to know it, too, because she stood up and offered to make them coffee. This time Luca didn't decline.

When she left the room, Luca went to Vin, wrapping his arms around him from behind. Vin didn't resist. He rested his head on Luca's chest, entwining their fingers over his stomach.

"You okay?" Luca asked, knowing it was a useless question, but he didn't know what else to say.

"No," Vin said with a sigh. "I don't know what to make of all this."

"You don't have to make anything out of it right now, *caro*. You have all the time in the world to think it through when we leave." Luca kissed Vin's temple, tightening his arms around him. "Don't be too hard on Maria. She's trying to help, and none of this is her fault."

Luca could see Maria's composure was slipping, too, and she needed a moment alone. This was hard on both of them. Maria must been carrying her own guilt, and it was plainly obvious she cared about Vin.

"She'd want to be a part of your life if you let her," Luca whispered against Vin's skin.

"What was stopping her before? Why didn't *she* get in touch with me if she cares so much?"

"Ask her."

Vin turned in Luca's arms, his beautiful face distorted in a tortured frown. Luca wished he could take the pain away, but he knew Vin had to do this on his own.

"Thank you," he said, pressing their lips together. It was a sweet, fleeting kiss, and it seemed to drain some of the tension from Vin's body.

They made their way back to the couch and sat down just as Maria returned with a tray full of aromatic coffees and sweets. Everyone made their coffees as they liked them and helped themselves to a couple of chocolate cookies, and instantly the atmosphere in the room changed.

KISS AND RIDE

Vin relaxed back in the couch, clutching his coffee mug in both hands, ready to ask the rest of his questions.

"Why didn't you get in touch with me? Especially after Mom died?" He asked, no accusation in his voice, only curiosity.

Maria faltered, obviously not expecting the question. "Antonio wouldn't let me," she said, avoiding Vin's gaze.

"You don't seem like a woman who cares what anyone thinks," Vin said, taking a sip of his coffee, his eyes fixed on his aunt.

She smiled. "I don't care what anyone thinks. But after Valentina passed, I had no way of getting in touch with you. He wouldn't give me any details where to find you." Her smile grew sad, then vanished. She licked her lips and Luca noticed she wasn't wearing any lipstick anymore. "I begged him to bring you here. I told him I'd take care of you, he wouldn't even know you were here." She shook her head, putting the mug back on the table.

"Why did he work so hard to keep me away?" Vin sounded more confused than angry, as if resigned to the idea he'd never be able to fix anything, rather, trying to understand, solve the puzzle his father'd been.

"He pushed everyone away. It was the way he was," Maria said. "God knows he tried to get rid of me, too, so many times. You have no idea the things he'd say to me, trying to hurt me so badly that I'd never come back. But I knew it was his mental illness talking. And," Maria swallowed hard, her lip trembling. "He was my brother. I couldn't leave him, we only had each other."

Every instinct Luca had told him Maria could use a hug right now, but he stayed put, watching for Vin's reaction. He didn't move, but his shoulders slumped and he bit his lip, glancing at Luca uncertainly.

Maria spoke before Vin had a chance to. "I don't know why he did it, any of it. Maybe he hated people seeing him this way, I don't know. But I know he cared about you, in his own way. I'm not trying to justify anything he did, and if you want to keep hating him nobody will hold it against you."

"I don't hate him," Vin blurted out. "I never did. I thought I did, *wished* I did, but I was mostly angry at him." Vin studied his coffee cup intently, not meeting his aunt's eyes. "I'd have given anything to spend a single day with him," he said softly.

It was Maria who stood up and came to Vin, sitting down on the couch next to him and wrapping a slender arm around his shoulders. She said something in his ear, too low for Luca to hear, but he saw Vin nodding.

The tone of the meeting changed after that. Vin asked a lot more questions, but more to do with getting to know his dad then the reasons why he'd chosen not to be a part of his life. Maria brought out several photo albums, telling Vin stories about Antonio, making Vin

KISS AND RIDE

smile. He held Luca's hand, pulling him closer, squeezing his fingers from time to time to reassure himself.

Luca was more than happy to provide the quiet support Vin needed. From the moment he'd laid eyes on him in that elevator, Luca'd hated the air of misery surrounding Vin, and he'd hated it even more today. But hearing Vin's laughter made the weight on his chest lift, letting him breathe easier.

Before they left, Maria gave Vin a gift wrapped in colorful Christmas paper. Vin tore into it eagerly and found a photo album of his own, full of pictures of Antonio. There were pictures of all three of them, too, Vin cute as a button, and his mother, an elegant and beautiful woman whose dark eyes sparkled with joy on every photo. Vin might look like his dad but he'd definitely inherited his mother's elegant pose.

At the door, Maria asked him to keep in touch and Vin promised he would. They hugged for a long moment, Vin's eyes shining with tears as he let go of his aunt.

"Did he know? About me? That I..." He faltered as if unsure how to phrase his question. "That I create things, too?"

Maria grinned, pulling him in for another hug. "He knew," she said with conviction. "He knew from the moment you were born."

Vin's eyes filled with tears. "Really?"

"Yes. He called me the day you were born and said, 'Maria, he's beautiful.'" Maria wiped the tear that rolled down Vin's cheek. "'I'm going to call him Vincent, after Van Gogh. Because he'll be one of the greats, I know it in my gut.'"

Vin hugged his aunt again and they stayed like that for a while, before she bid them goodbye and they walked down the stairs. In the lobby, Vin hesitated before pushing the front door open. Luca handed him a tissue, smiling as Vin wiped his tears, because this time they were happy tears.

Back in Luca's apartment, Vin felt as if he was floating. He'd felt like that ever since they'd left his aunt's place. Everything that he'd learned today was playing over and over in his head, not making much sense, but not letting his mind rest either. He needed some sort of anchor, some comforting weight to pull him back to the present moment, and make the whirlwind of thoughts slow down.

KISS AND RIDE

Luca sensed what he needed the second he locked the door behind them and met Vin's gaze. Pulling him in for a kiss, he backed Vin towards the bedroom where he took his time making Vin writhe underneath him, taking him to the edge, then bringing him slowly down until Vin was a gasping, squirming mess, unaware of anything else but the need in the pit of his stomach.

When Luca finally let him come, Vin was exhausted, but he'd never felt calmer. His mind was completely blank, probably for the first time in his entire life, and all he could do was roll on his stomach and pass out in a dreamless stupor.

A loud noise woke Vin with a start. Confused, he looked around the dark room but Luca was gone. Rolling on his back, Vin rubbed a hand over his face, trying to regain consciousness.

Bang.

There it was again. Throwing on his sweats and a t-shirt, Vin ventured out of the bedroom to find the source of the noise. He heard Luca's voice, letting out a string of curses, then another bang. He found him in the kitchen, palms on the counter, his chest rapidly rising and falling as if he couldn't get enough oxygen into his lungs. His head hung low, his shoulder blades sticking out through the thin t-shirt he wore.

And all around him lay broken pieces of plates, mugs, and whatever else had been on that counter.

"Luca?" Vin said, stepping inside the kitchen and closing the door behind him. "What's wrong?"

Luca turned towards him, his eyes red and his cheeks wet. "Fuck, sorry, didn't mean to wake you," he said, wiping his nose with the back of his hand.

Vin stepped closer, mindful of the broken pieces on the floor. He placed a hand on Luca's shoulder when he reached him, feeling him shaking underneath his palm.

"Tell me what's wrong."

"Got a call from my lawyer. My parents refused the offer I made them to buy them out. They want to appeal again, and considering it's their last chance, they won't stop at anything to get what they want."

Luca let out another string of curses, taking the few steps to the chair and falling into it. His head rolled against the back of the chair and he stared at the ceiling as he spoke.

"Why are they doing this, Vin? Why are they punishing me for who I am?" Vin had no answer to this question. Instead, he walked to Luca's chair and started massaging his stiff shoulders without a comment. "It's not enough that they gave me up, that I have no family because of them, but they also want to take away my dreams." Vin kept kneading Luca's shoulders, glad when Luca made an appreciative sound, sitting up in the chair to give Vin better access to his back. "I'm so fucking tired," he said with a sad sigh. "So sick and tired of swimming against the current, of fighting and fighting, and never getting a break. Sometimes I feel I should just give up and let them have the fucking house, and be done with it all."

"You can't do that," Vin said, anger blossoming in his chest. He let go of Luca's shoulders and stepped around the chair to straddle his thighs. "You can't." Luca wrapped his arms around Vin's waist and gazed in his eyes with resignation. "It's your dream and you'll fight for it however long it takes." Luca didn't seem convinced, he rested his forehead on Vin's chest, and Vin buried his fingers in his hair. "It was your grandmother's wish for you to have that house, Luca. She knew you were the one she could trust to take care of it, to make it what it once was. You owe it to her to keep fighting."

Luca raised his head and stared at Vin as if seeing him for the first time. His dark eyes were full of so much sorrow, so much pain, that Vin's heart clenched in sympathy.

"You're right," Luca said, licking his dry lips.

Vin kissed him, wrapping an arm around Luca's shoulders and pulling him close. Luca's fingers dug into his hips as he kissed him back, lips sucking, teeth clashing, mouths eager for more. Vin loved the feel of Luca's beard against his skin, craved it, rubbing his cheek against it when Luca's lips moved to kiss along his jaw.

"You fucked me senseless two hours ago, and I still want you," Vin said, arching his back to give Luca better access to his throat. "What are you doing to me?"

"Same thing you're doing to me, *tesoro*," Luca said, grabbing Vin's ass and lifting him off the chair as he stood up. Vin wrapped his legs tighter around Luca's waist and let him carry him back to the bedroom.

Vin pulled the heavy glass door open and held it for Luca as they walked into the offices of *Bianchi & Donati*. Today was the reading of the will. Vin'd asked Luca to go with him – he couldn't face it alone. God, he had no idea what he would have done if he hadn't met Luca. He'd be a mess in some hostel, crying himself to

KISS AND RIDE

sleep every night, probably still too angry to even consider talking to Maria, and so fucking lost that he wouldn't know how to find his way back.

Luca'd said he'd wished for Vin, but Luca had turned out to be Vin's own Christmas miracle.

The receptionist took their names and gave them visitor badges, then pointed them in the direction of meeting room two. Vin thanked her, trying to keep his composure as they walked down the hall. His stomach was churning, his palms were sweating, and he was so nervous he thought he might puke.

The thing was, he had no idea what to expect. The lawyer, Lorenzo Donati, had told him he absolutely had to be present at the reading of the will as Antonio's main beneficiary, but in all honesty Vin couldn't care less about it. He didn't want his father's money or whatever he had left him. He felt like a fraud, swooping in at the last moment to grab the prize, when in fact he hadn't even known his own father.

But that had been Antonio's choice, not his. And Vin was working on forgiving him.

They reached the heavy oak door of meeting room two, but didn't immediately enter. Vin hesitated, taking a few deep breaths to calm down. Luca entwined their fingers, squeezing them gently, his dark eyes full of empathy when Vin looked at him.

"It'll be alright, *carino*," he said, giving him a kind smile.

Vin felt his nerves calm a little as if Luca was injecting some of his own strength in him. He pressed his lips to Luca's, a quick, gentle kiss to reassure himself, and then pushed the door open.

The room was huge, with floor to ceiling windows, elegantly decorated in neutral colors and minimalistic furnishings, a large table with chairs all around it taking up most of the space. Every chair was currently occupied by men and women dressed in sharp suits, leaving only two seats empty for Vin and Luca. The only bright spot among the black and navy suits was Maria, dressed in a light blue dress, an extravagant necklace around her neck. She smiled when she saw them, but didn't otherwise react.

"Vincent, hello, good to see you again," Lorenzo Donati said as he stood up from his seat at the front of the table and rushed to shake Vin's hand. Much like at the memorial service, the lawyer was impeccably dressed in a black tailored suit, the color complementing his kind brown eyes. "And you must be Luca?" Luca nodded, shaking the lawyer's hand in turn.

Vin had emailed the evening before asking if he could bring Luca along. He hadn't been sure how these things went, if it wasn't a private event, family only allowed. He didn't want to drag Luca along only to have to leave him to wait in the lobby. To his relief, Donati had replied almost instantly, assuring him it was perfectly fine to be accompanied by a close friend for emotional support.

KISS AND RIDE

And now, looking at all these people who didn't seem like they had anything in common with his father, Vin started to feel nervous all over again.

"Please, take your seats and let's begin," Donati said, walking back to his own chair.

Donati had a stack of papers in front of him, but before he started on the will itself he explained he was Antonio Alesi's personal lawyer and had been handling his estate for over fifteen years. He'd been a close friend, too, and was deeply saddened by Antonio's sudden passing.

There were no more personal speeches after that. The will was pretty straightforward – a lot of Antonio's art was going to different galleries and museums around the world, donated by him with a no-reselling clause. Vin started to make sense of all the suits in the room. They must have been representatives of the mentioned galleries.

When all that was sorted, Donati moved on to read the rest of Antonio's will. Maria Alesi received a substantial sum of money plus some of Antonio's favorite pieces, to do whatever she wished with them. And then it was Vin's turn. Antonio had no other family apart from his sister and his son, so all eyes in the room turned towards him.

Vin flushed, feeling like a bug under a microscope. His instinct was to jump from his seat and run, but thankfully he still had some control over his overactive mind, and managed to calm down enough to remain seated. Luca's hand found his under the table, and Vin squeezed it to a point that must have been painful, but Luca didn't pull away.

Antonio had wished for Vin to have his apartment in Rome and everything that was in it. With a note of annoyance, Donati explained that Antonio had explicitly forbidden anyone from entering the apartment after his death, so everything was as he left it. Vin also received the remaining balance in all of Antonio's accounts, access to his safety deposit boxes, and the exclusive rights to all of Antonio's art pieces that weren't already donated.

Vin's head was spinning, the lawyer's words jumbling in his mind. He needed time to process all this information, and not just the fact that he'd become a very rich man overnight. What was giving him the most anxiety was the fact that he'd have to go to his father's apartment, see it as he'd left it, feel his presence in there in all his things. Vin was nowhere near ready to do that.

When the reading was over and all the suits left, chatting excitedly about their newly acquired priceless pieces of art, Maria came to Vin and gave him a long hug, reminding him he could always call her when he needed to talk. She then kissed Luca on both cheeks and left.

"If you'd like to follow me, I have something for you in my office," Donati said, gesturing to Vin and Luca to follow.

KISS AND RIDE

God, when was this going to be over? What more surprises had his father left for him? Vin wasn't sure he could take any more.

In his office, the lawyer walked to his desk and pulled out a large leather folder from one of the drawers.

"All the information you'll need to access your father's accounts is in these documents," he said, pointing to the folder. "I'll need you to sign a few things so that we can move forward and transfer all accounts and legal documents in your name." He paused, studying Vin, frowning when Vin didn't react. "Your father really was a close friend of mine, Vincent," Donati said, his frown relaxing. "If you ever need anything, anything at all, here or in New York, you can call me any time and I'll sort it out for you. I hope, in time, you'll learn to trust me, just like your father did."

A thought flashed in Vin's mind, making his eyes widen. He voiced it before he could think better of it.

"Were you the one who arranged for me to be placed with the Browns?"

Donati tried to school his features but something sad and painful passed in his eyes before he could manage.

"Yes," he said. "The Browns were the best fostering family I could find. They only had one more kid, and I made sure they didn't get any more. Antonio didn't want you to feel neglected in a bigger family."

"But..." Vin stammered, not really sure how to form his questions.

His four years with the Browns had been great – you couldn't find a more wholesome American family if you tried. Best of all was that he stayed in New York City; he wouldn't have been able to bear moving out of the city he'd grown up in and loved. The other foster kid the Browns had, Michael, was Vin's age, and they'd gotten along really well. Michael had moved to LA to pursue an acting career, and it'd become more and more difficult to keep in touch, but they still called and emailed from time to time.

Luca's hand on his arm brought Vin back from his thoughts and he found the lawyer staring at him patiently, waiting for Vin's questions.

"How did you do that?" Vin finally asked.

"I know people in the right places," Donati said with a grin and a wink, breaking the awkward moment. He pulled a drawer on his desk open and took out a set of keys, placing them on the desk. "These are the keys to Antonio's apartment." He pushed them gently towards Vin when he didn't move to take them. "I can't do anything before you go in there yourself, Vincent. I'm not going to break Antonio's trust on this. So, when you're ready..."

"No," Vin said, flinching away from the keys. "I have four more days left in Rome before I have to go

KISS AND RIDE

back to New York. I don't think that's enough time for me to come to terms with everything, let alone go to my father's apartment."

Donati studied Vin, his brows drawing down. "Either way, take the keys. They're yours. Whenever you decide to use them."

Vin took the fucking keys and dropped them in his pocket as if they'd burned him. He'd made enough of a fool of himself today, there was no need for any more embarrassment.

Thankfully, the lawyer didn't mention the apartment anymore. He set the documents Vin needed to sign in front of him, explaining each of them carefully, answering any questions Vin had. That done, he shook both Vin and Luca's hands and let them out of his office.

Outside, Vin could take a deep breath to fill his lungs for the first time today. He'd never felt more trapped in his entire life, not even when he'd been stuck in that elevator with Luca.

"I think *gelato* is in order," Luca said, reaching for Vin's hand.

Vin smiled at him, ridiculously glad Luca didn't want to discuss anything that had happened today.

"And a shot of tequila," Vin said, grabbing Luca's outstretched hand.

"I think I know a place that serves both."

Luca's heart ached as he watched Vin withdraw into himself after they left the lawyers' offices. He claimed to be fine, and just needed time to process everything, but the smile didn't reach his eyes anymore. Luca gave him space, and would readily open his arms when Vin wanted to snuggle, but wouldn't keep him there when he wanted to sulk and sketch in his notebook.

He'd done that all day. Drawing. He'd only sought Luca out when he came to bed, the intensity of his touch burning Luca's skin. They'd had sex like never before, Vin's raw desire sucking the air out of the room, making Luca feel every move, every touch, every gasp and moan as if there was an electric current between them, zapping and snipping at his every nerve.

Exhausted, they'd fallen asleep in each other's arms, but when Luca woke in the middle of the night, the bed was empty next to him. Padding barefoot on the cold floor, Luca found Vin curled on the sofa, a blanket over his shoulders, the only light in the room coming from the lights on the Christmas tree. He had his notepad in his lap, a pencil hanging between his fingers, but he was staring at the changing blinking pattern of the lights, his drawing forgotten.

Luca leaned against the door frame.

"Hey," he said softly, but it still startled Vin. He dropped the pencil when he jumped a little, his blue eyes changing shade every few seconds as the lights kept blinking. "You okay?" Luca had asked that question way too many times.

Vin shook his head wordlessly, bending down to pick up his pencil. Luca walked over to him, sitting down on the couch, and to his surprise Vin offered him to snuggle under the blanket with him. Resting his head on Vin's shoulder, Luca watched as he kept drawing, the pencil moving swiftly over the paper creating sharp angles and harsh curves that didn't immediately translate into a particular shape in Luca's mind. Looking closer, Luca recognized the shape of a tree in the center of the drawing, and lots of small shapes underneath it. The whole picture was very abstract, striking in its originality.

"The apple doesn't fall far from the tree," Vin said, his voice quiet and hoarse.

And suddenly his whole drawing made sense.

"Everything I fucking do reminds me of him," Vin continued, his hand moving rapidly on the paper as he talked. "My looks, my talent, my last name, being here, being in New York, speaking Italian..." His hand stilled on the paper and he dropped the pencil, burying his face in his hands. "He's everywhere around me, all the time, and yet I barely know him."

Luca pulled him in until Vin rested his head on his chest.

"You know..." Luca began, but hesitated, not sure how Vin would react to his words. "You can get to know him a bit better, even if not in person."

Vin lifted his head off Luca's chest, his brows furrowing.

"You do have the keys to his apartment. And the lawyer said it was as your dad had left it. I bet there's a lot to learn about the man Antonio Alesi was in there. And you can always talk to Maria, ask her to tell you more about him."

Vin's gaze lost its focus and he snuggled back into Luca. He hadn't flat out refused, which Luca considered a good sign.

A few minutes passed before Vin sat up, offered Luca his hand and pulled him off the couch. They lay in Luca's bed, Vin curled around him, his breathing growing heavier as Luca stroked his back.

KISS AND RIDE

Vin woke up in a much better mood than Luca expected considering the few hours he'd slept. Luca made them breakfast and was surprised that Vin didn't protest when Luca suggested they spend the day walking around Rome. They could both use the fresh air and the distraction.

It was a sunny day, but much colder than it had been recently. The sky was a crisp, cloudless blue, and Luca pulled his sunglasses over his eyes while at the same time buttoning his coat all the way up. Vin was quiet walking next to him, but he didn't seem upset anymore. There was an air of peace around him, as if he was done fighting and was ready to move on.

They walked aimlessly around, enjoying the chilly, sunny day, browsing the independent boutiques and endless souvenir shops. Vin's mood got considerably better when he found a grey cashmere sweater that he loved, and it turned out it was on sale. He walked out of the boutique with a huge smile on his face, wrapping Luca's a bit tighter around his neck as a shiver ran through him.

Deciding it was time to have a little rest and warm up a bit, Luca led them to a cosy coffee shop where they shared a plate of pastries and enjoyed aromatic coffees. Vin talked animatedly about his studies, about New York, about his friends, and his colleagues at the gallery. Luca loved seeing Vin like this, free and happy, and present in the moment. His eyes sparkled in the purest shade of blue, and it took all of Luca's willpower not to drag Vin over the table and kiss him senseless.

After lunch, Vin wanted to buy some souvenirs to take back home. Luca's heart jittered at the thought of Vin leaving in three days, their wonderful, warm cocoon broken forever. He'd known from the start Vin was a temporary distraction, a fleeting moment in time that would be over all too soon. But what he hadn't known was that he'd feel this disappointed when it was time to part ways.

"Are these what I think they are?" Vin said, leaning in Luca's space to whisper theatrically in his ear.

Luca followed his line of sight. "Yes."

Vin's eyes grew wide as he walked closer to a selection of souvenir magnets and ogled the ones that were a pretty accurate 3D reproduction of David's dick.

"Only in Italy would someone think it's appropriate to butcher Michelangelo's David," he said, shaking his head, but a smile pulled at the corners of his mouth. "And look, there're different shapes. And some of them are even painted in the Italian flag colors!" Vin turned to look at Luca, his cheeks dimpled in a grin.

Luca's heart stuttered, then exploded in his chest.

"Yes," Luca said, trying to disperse the nagging thoughts and feelings currently fogging his mind. He cleared his throat. "These are quite common here, they have them in every souvenir shop."

KISS AND RIDE

"What's with Italians and dicks? Souvenirs, pasta, postcards, sculptures..." Vin mused, counting them off on his fingers.

"There's nothing wrong with a nice, thick dick, is there?" Luca whispered in Vin's ear, and felt as a shiver ran through Vin's body.

"Nope, definitely not," Vin said, collecting all the David's dick magnets from the display and taking them inside the shop to pay for them.

Luca laughed, shaking his head when Vin turned to wink at him over his shoulder. He returned a few minutes later carrying a bag of stuff which suspiciously didn't look like just the magnets. With a cheeky smile he opened the bag and showed Luca a calendar with sexy men dressed as gladiators, bookmarks with the whole statue of David, and a book with all kinds of naked male statues in different stages of arousal.

"At least there's a theme to your gifts," Luca said, arching an eyebrow.

"Right?" Vin beamed at him as if Luca had uncovered some ancient secret. "Now I only need a few packets of that penis shaped pasta and I'm all set."

The ice rink had been Vin's idea.

As they'd neared *Castel Sant'Angelo* they'd heard live music and headed in that direction. A rock band seemed to be doing an impromptu jam session in front of the museum, a crowd already gathered around them. Vin'd snuggled in Luca's arms as they listened to the music, tapping his foot in rhythm with the bass. It was getting dark by then, the street lamps flickering to life, as well as the many festive lights and decorations everywhere around them.

On their way back, Vin'd spotted the ice rink and his eyes had grown wide with excitement. So, of course, Luca had agreed to go ice skating even if he was crap at it. Just as he was putting his ice skates on, his phone rang in his pocket.

"Hey," Marco's smooth voice came from the other end. "What are you up to?"

"Ice skating," Luca said with a heavy sigh.

"For real? But you suck!"

"I really *really* do."

Marco chuckled. "The New Yorker still with you?"

Marco had texted Luca with a million questions after he'd dropped off their Christmas tree. Luca had given him as little information as possible, trying to shut him up, but not willing to discuss his spur of the moment relationship with Vin yet.

"Yes," Luca said tersely, hoping to get his friend off his back.

"Good. I'm free this evening and I'm going to join you at the rink, and then we can grab a bite to eat, yeah?"

Luca's jaw dropped open but before he could find a less offensive way to get rid of Marco, he'd hung up with a cheerful, "See you in a bit."

"Luca? You alright?" Vin called.

Luca realized he'd been staring at his phone long after Marco'd hung up on him, and looked up to see Vin, elbows propped on the rail, his cheeks already rosy from doing a couple of laps while Luca struggled with tying his ice skates.

"Yeah, I'm fine," he said, waving his hand dismissively. "I'll be right there."

Easier said than done. Luca'd last skated when he was a kid. Even then it hadn't been a pretty sight. He waddled to the opening in the side boards and nearly fell down on his back the moment the skates' blades touched the ice.

This was going to be a fucking nightmare.

Out of nowhere, Vin appeared next to him, a smile playing on his lips as he offered Luca his hand. Beggars couldn't be choosers. Luca grabbed Vin's hand, his only chance of staying on his feet, and let Vin guide him on the ice, carefully avoiding all the other people. As they glided on the ice, Vin offered pieces of advice like, 'bend your knees', 'push your feet at a forty five degree angle', and 'squat down a little', and soon Luca was skating nearly on his own. He didn't let go of

Vin's hand because he was still not very good at stopping, but other than that he could glide on the ice without falling all on his own.

When flopping down and embarrassing himself in front of five year old children who skated as if they were at the Olympics wasn't such a great possibility anymore, Luca relaxed and let his senses come back to life. He heard the cheerful Christmas songs coming from the speakers; saw the colorful Christmas tree with blinking lights and fake presents right outside the rink; smelled the signature scent of the ice mixed with the enticing aroma of fresh coffee and pastries.

He felt Vin's soft, warm hand in his, patiently guiding him through every obstacle in their way.

"Hey! You're skating!" Marco's voice boomed right behind Luca, making him lose his balance. Vin grabbed his upper arm and steadied it, propping him next to the railing.

"Fucking hell, man, you startled me!" Luca said, his heart thumping.

Marco didn't seem to care he'd almost caused Luca to fall down on the hard ice, probably dragging Vin with him. He grinned at Vin and shook his hand, then sped off to do laps around the rink.

"Go," Luca said, waving a hand after Marco. "Have some fun. I think I need to sit down anyway." Luca's legs were killing him from all that squatting and bending and gliding.

"Are you sure?"

KISS AND RIDE

Luca nodded, then made his way towards the tiny door, taking a deep breath as the ground underneath his skates became stable. Sitting in one of the chairs, he exhaled a deep breath and leaned back, content just to watch Vin and Marco as they skated gracefully together.

Marco gestured wildly as he spoke, and Vin's grin never left his face, a few times he actually had to stop and grab the railing he was laughing so hard. Luca smiled to himself. Marco was probably telling him embarrassing stories about Luca, but he didn't care. He loved seeing that unguarded grin on Vin's face, the way his shoulders shook and his cheeks dimpled as he laughed.

After they got tired showing off their ice skating skills, Vin and Marco joined Luca outside and together they went to have dinner. Marco's favorite place was close to the rink, so they headed that way and were soon seated in the warm, cosy restaurant. Luca had been right – Marco'd been telling Vin stories about him. Greatly embellished stories. He kept doing so at dinner, making them both laugh. Luca had forgotten how much fun his best friend was – he rarely saw him anymore. He rarely saw anyone or did anything but work anymore.

"So then, the lead singer runs off to the toilet and starts puking his guts out! It's obvious he can't go on performing and we still have five songs left in our set. The whole pub is full of people, staring at us, whispering to each other, speculating what's going on," Marco said, taking a sip of his wine. Vin watched him with hooded eyes, twinkling from the two glasses of wine he'd already had. "Enter my knight in shining armor!" He said with flourish, gesturing to Luca. "Just as I was thinking of pulling the microphone to my piano and singing the rest of the fucking set, Luca jumps on stage, apologizes for the unexpected events and waves at us to start the next song!"

"What was I supposed to do? You were all frozen in place, staring at each other with these wide, unblinking eyes, it was embarrassing!" Luca said, shaking his head at the memory. "It was one of your first gigs, I had to do something or nobody would have ever invited you again."

"Were you any good?" Vin asked, raising an eyebrow in challenge.

"Oh my god, he was incredible!" Marco exclaimed, making both Luca and Vin laugh. "He took off his leather jacket and was wearing a tight white t-shirt underneath. All the women started making bedroom eyes at him even before he started singing."

"He's lying," Luca said with a sigh.

"I'm not! You totally did that on purpose so that they'd like you even if you sounded bad!" Luca shook his head again and grinned at Vin.

"What kind of music do you play?" Vin asked.

"Alternative rock," Marco said proudly.

Kiss and Ride

Vin's smile widened and he leaned forward, placing his elbows on the table.

"When I first saw you I thought you looked like you were in a boyband."

Luca burst out laughing, and Marco's mouth gaped open in outrage.

"What?" Vin said, looking at them with mock innocence. "That's a compliment, dude. Take it and run."

Back at Luca's apartment, tipsy and eager to get each other naked, Vin ripped a few buttons from Luca's shirt, no patience left to unbutton it all the way. Luca didn't even care. He had three nights left with Vin and he wasn't going to lose a single second worrying about anything else but how to make Vin scream his name.

Luca heard the music before they'd even reached the building. Marco'd invited them to a New Year's Eve party at their friend Giovanni's place, and even though Luca would much rather spend the next two days in bed with Vin, he didn't want to miss out on catching up with his friends either. He hadn't been home during the holidays in years, so, at the time, Marco's invitation had seemed like a good idea. Plus, Vin'd seemed eager to do something on New Year's, too.

A wall of sound and color assaulted his senses when Giovanni opened the door of his apartment and welcomed them in with hugs and kisses on both cheeks. What followed was a whirlwind of dancing, drinking, laughing with his friends, making out with Vin as they danced around the huge Christmas tree Giovanni had somehow managed to drag to his apartment on the fifth floor.

Vin always looked gorgeous, but tonight he was hot as fuck. Black skinny jeans hugged his ass perfectly, and a tight Guns N' Roses t-shirt with cut off sleeves displayed his toned arms covered in tattoos. As usual, his wild hair was pulled back in a bun on the back of his head, and looking at it Luca couldn't wait until they got back home and he could rip the elastic band, running his fingers through the soft curls.

"You've got it bad, *amico*," Marco said, leaning on the wall next to Luca.

Luca rolled his eyes, taking a sip of his plastic cup full of rum and coke.

KISS AND RIDE

"Deny it all you want, but the way you're looking at him says it all," Marco said, hiding his smirk as he brought his own plastic cup to his lips.

"It's not like that," Luca said weakly, trying to come up with an explanation what this thing between them actually was.

"I've known you for nearly ten years and I've never seen you look at anyone like that, not even that guy you considered asking to move in with you, what was his name?"

"Rafael."

"Yes. Rafael. The personal trainer." Marco waggled his eyebrows at Luca as if he'd said 'porn star'.

"It doesn't matter," Luca said with a heavy sigh, drowning the last of his drink in one big gulp. "He's leaving the day after tomorrow."

Luca's eyes followed Vin around the room, watching him as he danced and laughed with Luca's friends who – much like Luca – had accepted him as one of their own without question. Vin had that air about him, that presence that drew people in and it was impossible to resist his charm.

Marco sighed theatrically next to Luca. "All that angst is ruining my mood," he said with an exaggerated eye roll. "You know this doesn't have to be the end. He's looking at you with the same hooded sex eyes as you give him all the time, so I'm pretty sure he feels the same way."

"He's not..." Luca began but Marco lifted a hand to silence him and continued.

"Whatever. I don't get the angst you're going through right now because it's obvious that you both feel the same way and can make it work if you want to." Marco paused to take a sip of his drink, but Luca knew he wouldn't be allowed to protest even if he tried, so he kept his mouth shut. "But even if you only have two days left together stop fucking sulking in the corner and go be with him."

Marco patted Luca's arm and stalked off, leaving him alone. Luca glared after him. It was so easy for him to say these things, oversimplify the situation. Luca hadn't managed to have a relationship with anyone in his home town for longer than a couple of months, let alone anyone who lived on another continent. It just wasn't in the cards for them, and no amount of agonizing over it would help. At least Marco was right about one thing – he could go enjoy his remaining time with Vin instead of sulking in the corner.

They danced together until the music stopped and Giovanni announced they'd be doing the countdown to the new year soon. Everyone hurried to refill their plastic cups and be ready for the celebration once the clock struck midnight.

Luca pulled Vin closer, leading him to a secluded corner of the room where they wouldn't be pushed and jostled when everyone got a bit too excited

KISS AND RIDE

over the arrival of the new year. Vin went willingly, snuggling in Luca's arms, staring into his eyes as everyone around them counted the last seconds before midnight. Luca couldn't look away. There was nothing around him to look at but Vin. He held him captive in those blue eyes, and Luca wondered what he was thinking. A small crease appeared between Vin's brows before he closed his eyes and sought Luca's lips with his.

Lost in their kiss, Luca barely registered as cheers and whistles erupted around them. The only way he wanted to celebrate was kissing Vin, touching him, burying himself deep in Vin's body until time stopped and they could stay like this forever.

"Let's go home," Luca murmured against Vin's lips.

When Luca woke up the next morning, Vin wasn't sleeping next to him. He'd snuck out earlier, after Luca felt him tossing and turning for most of the night.

Something was bothering Vin if he couldn't fall asleep after being utterly exhausted the night before.

On the way to the bathroom, Luca could smell something cooking and hear the coffee brewing in the machine. It was such a domestic thing to do, and yet so out of reach for Luca. He barely slept in his own bed anymore, let alone have someone cook him breakfast on the weekend.

With a sad shake of his head, he walked into the bathroom, closing the door behind him with the resolve that he'd make the most of today without thinking about tomorrow.

"I want to go to my dad's place today," Vin said after they finished their breakfast and took their coffees to the living room. "Will you come with me?"

Luca frowned. He was glad Vin had decided to go, he knew he wouldn't have been able to stop thinking about it had he gone back to New York without setting foot in his father's apartment. But it felt so intrusive to

KISS AND RIDE

go with him. Did Vin really want a witness to this private moment?

He wouldn't have asked if he didn't want you to go, dumbass.

Right.

"Please?" Vin added in a small voice when Luca didn't immediately reply.

"Of course," Luca said, reaching for Vin's hand. "If you want me there I'll be there."

Vin clasped Luca's fingers and they finished their coffees as they watched the news.

Antonio's apartment took the last two floors of a well-kept building on *Via San Teodoro*, right in the heart of Rome's historic center. Vin's hand shook as he tried to figure out which key went into which lock, until he gave up and thrust the bunch of keys into Luca's hand. With considerably less trouble, Luca unlocked the door and held it open for Vin.

Inside, the place was dark and smelled of old paint fumes, dust and some sort of chemical Luca couldn't identify. Vin took a few tentative steps inside, his eyes wide, as if he was expecting something to jump out at him from any corner.

"I think we'll see better if we open the shutters on the windows," Luca said. "And maybe let some fresh air in?"

Vin nodded, still looking around in a daze. Luca made his way to the nearest window, pulled the curtains and opened it, then unlocked the wooden shutters and pushed them open, too. Bright light flooded in the apartment, making the dust bunnies even more noticeable.

The view from the window was breathtaking – the building was on top of a hill overlooking Rome's historic center, and being on the fourth floor Luca could easily see the Roman Forum as well as several churches, museums, and historic buildings.

"Wow," Vin said behind him, coming to rest his chin on Luca's shoulder. "That's some view."

They admired the beauty of Rome for a few more minutes before Vin took a deep breath and headed to the room across the hall. Luka followed him into what looked like a living room. There wasn't much to it – a couple of sofas, top of the range TV and sound system, a few paintings on the walls. It looked like nobody had used that room for a long time. Vin didn't linger there. He kept walking in and out of rooms, his eyes scanning his surroundings as if looking for something in particular. Luca stuck his head in most rooms, but they looked quite impersonal, even if immaculately furnished. Apart from the living room, most were bedrooms, and the kitchen and dining room.

"His studio is probably upstairs," Vin said, looking at the staircase at the end of the corridor. "I'm pretty sure he rarely left it, so that's where we're going to find all his stuff. This place here looks like nobody's ever lived in it." He spread his arms wide indicating the whole first floor.

Luca had to agree. They climbed the stairs to the second floor where the chemical and paint smell got stronger. Vin gingerly opened the first door on the left, and after taking a quick peek, strode inside to open the window. When the light burst into the room, Luca saw it was nearly bare apart from a couple of chairs, a chest of drawers with all sorts of paint cans haphazardly thrown on top of it, dry paint splattered all over the floor.

And then there were the paintings. Piles and piles of paintings propped against the walls.

"My god," Vin said, raising a trembling hand to his mouth.

Walking over to the closest pile, Vin ran his hand along the lines of the top painting, his eyes filling with tears. He whirled around, scanning the room, looking so fucking lost it made Luca's breath catch.

Running out of the room, Vin started opening door after door, some sort of madness descending over him that Luca could only watch. In every room there were piles of paintings, sculptures, books and art supplies, carving materials, misshapen stones waiting to be turned into something beautiful, heaps of metal wire in all kinds of colors. In one of the rooms Luca saw a mattress on the floor, the bedding carelessly thrown aside.

Antonio Alesi, one of the most famous artists in contemporary culture, had slept on the floor of his studio, so deeply buried in his art that he rarely left it.

Luca was overwhelmed with sadness and pity for this great talent, this extraordinary man who had obviously been deeply troubled. He couldn't even begin to imagine how Vin must feel seeing all this, realizing the full extent of his father's condition.

Luca heard a sob coming from one of the rooms behind him and he hurried to see what was going on. He found Vin sitting cross-legged on the dirty floor, a thick notebook in his lap. When he reached him, Luca sat down next to him, wrapping an arm around his shoulders. Vin leaned back into his touch, but he kept crying silently as he read his father's handwriting. The top of the page said 'To my son' and from what Luca could see it was a personal essay about why Antonio had chosen to keep Vin away from his madness, as he'd called it himself. When Vin turned the page Luca gasped – the drawing that took nearly the entire page was of a man, his body distorted in pain as ghosts and demons flew all around him, pulling at his clothes, shouting at him, taunting him.

KISS AND RIDE

Vin closed the notebook with a thud, burying his face in Luca's chest. He stroked his back as he cried, and they sat there for what seemed like an eternity, but Luca didn't want to be anywhere else in the world right now.

Luca was reading a book in the living room when Vin opened the door.

"Hey," he said, coming to sit next to him on the couch.

He'd gone to bed straight after they'd come back this afternoon. Poor guy had been emotionally and physically exhausted. Looking at him, Luca thought he seemed better. His eyes were still a bit red and his hair was a mess, but at least he didn't look so goddamn miserable anymore.

"Hey yourself." Luca pulled him in his arms and kissed him, their lips lingering against each other. "Feel better?"

"Yeah." He chewed on his lip for a while before speaking again. "I'm going to call the lawyer tomorrow and ask him to take care of everything in the apartment.

Put it in storage for now. I have no idea what to do with all this art and I need some time to process everything." He sighed, then rubbed his eyes.

Luca'd seen him taking his father's notebook, but that was the only thing he'd taken from the apartment. The art alone probably cost a small fortune.

"I think that's a good idea," Luca said.

Vin lay his head in Luca's lap, staring at the ceiling. Luca raked his fingers through his hair, massaging the scalp, patiently waiting for Vin to say whatever was on his mind.

"I read some more from the notebook," he said. Luca hummed encouragingly. "I can't even imagine what he went through every single day. I still don't approve of his decision to keep me away, but I think I'm starting to get his logic behind it."

"He seemed like a deeply troubled man."

Vin looked content to simply lie in Luca's lap, letting his thoughts roam free as Luca's fingers relaxed his body.

His stomach rumbled, the sound strikingly loud in the quiet room. Luca laughed, letting Vin sit up, and they headed to the kitchen to make dinner.

KISS AND RIDE

Lying in bed, Luca watched as Vin gathered his things and arranged them in his suitcase. It was getting hard to breathe. Panic settled in his chest, suffocating him, and yet he tried to look normal on the outside. They talked and joked while Vin packed, as if it wasn't their last night together. As if tomorrow everything wouldn't change. As if the best thing that had happened to Luca in his entire life wasn't slipping through his fingers.

As if he wasn't letting it all happen.

Some of his thoughts must have shown on his face because Vin stopped what he was doing and crawled on the bed, settling between Luca's legs.

"You okay?" He asked, his gaze penetrating Luca's soul.

No, he wasn't fucking okay.

"Yeah. Why?" Luca's voice came out as a raspy whisper.

"You look sad."

Luca puffed out a long breath. "Of course I'm sad, Vin. You're leaving tomorrow."

As if the confirmation was all Vin needed, he closed the space between them, smashing their mouths together. Luca's arms came around him as he flipped them over, his body pressing Vin into the mattress. The desperation behind their kiss was palpable, and neither of them could hide it anymore. Vin had pretended he wasn't affected by his leaving tomorrow while he packed, but his mouth on Luca's told another story. He pulled at Luca's clothes, ripping seams and not caring, fingers digging in bare skin until they left red marks. Luca's teeth sank in the junction of Vin's neck, but instead of pulling away Vin craved it, exposing his neck even further. Biting, licking, sucking – Luca left as many marks on him as he could, hoping, *needing*, to let Vin go knowing he carried some part of Luca with him.

"Fuck, harder," Vin cried out, a loud moan tearing out of him as Luca sucked on his skin harder, leaving an angry purple bruise behind.

They ripped at each other's clothes quickly, impatient to feel skin against bare skin, Vin's back arching off the bed when Luca snuck his hand between them and fisted both their cocks.

"I'm close," he said, pushing Vin's hand away.

The need in his eyes said it all. He wanted Luca inside him, wanted to feel that explosion of pleasure when Luca's cock rubbed at his prostate. Wanted to come while Luca fucked him, claiming him, making him moan and twist and beg until the need inside him was satisfied.

Luca wanted all these things, too.

Hands shaking, Luca put the condom on and applied a generous amount of lube on both himself and Vin. He had no restraint to be patient right now, but he still needed to make sure he didn't hurt Vin. Wrapping at arm around his waist, Luca flipped them over, Vin straddling his thighs. With a sinful smirk, Vin placed his palms on Luca's chest and rolled his hips, Luca's cock hot and hard between his cheeks. He bent down, touching his lips to Luca's, coaxing them gently open with his tongue. As they kissed, Luca slowly pushed inside him, swallowing Vin's hoarse cry. Their hearts beat frantically against one another, their bodies joined together, nothing separating them anymore.

Vin made a strangled sound at the back of his throat and pulled back, propping his hands on both sides of Luca's head. Luca palmed his ass, urging him to move. Rolling his hips agonisingly slow, Vin ignored him, setting his own rhythm. His cock was trapped between their bodies, rubbing between their bellies, making Vin's eyes roll back.

Sitting up, Vin changed the angle and started bouncing on top of Luca faster, his moans getting louder, his hard cock bobbing up and down, precome dripping down his length. Luca reached for it, wrapping his fingers around it, jerking it in time with Vin's rhythm. With a hoarse cry, Vin came all over Luca's hand, his stomach, and his chest, his whole body taunt, lean muscles straining, soft skin covered in a sheen of sweat and colorful tattoos.

The beautiful sight of Vin coming on top of him nearly did Luca in. He let go of his cock, pulling Vin down for a kiss, grabbing his ass in both hands as they kissed. Vin whimpered against his lips as Luca started thrusting his hips up in a desperate, unsteady rhythm, the pressure building, tingling inside him. Vin's moans became louder, more urgent, his kisses biting, his touch nearly painful as he dug his fingers in Luca's chest, urging him to go faster, deeper, until they both couldn't stand it anymore.

Later, after a lazy shower, they enjoyed each other's bodies slower, more gently, kissing over every red mark and purple bruise their frantic fucking had caused.

Sleep didn't come easy after that. They were both bone tired, but wide awake. Vin lay his head on Luca's chest, listening to his heart beating as he traced his ribs over and over. Ordinarily, that would have calmed Luca enough to fall asleep, but not tonight. He didn't want to miss a second in Vin's presence even if it meant staying awake all night. He'd sleep tomorrow when there was nobody keeping him awake anymore.

"I don't want you to go," he said, surprising himself. That thought had been circling on a loop in his mind for days, but he'd never planned on voicing it.

Vin lifted his head and met his eyes. In the darkness they looked black, but Luca could still see the moisture in them.

"I don't want to go either," he said, making Luca's heart both soar and break at the same time. "But it's not the right time for us, Luca. I have to finish my degree and deal with everything that's happened with my dad, and I need to do that on my own. I need to figure out what to do with my life.

"I've never had a dream. I've always had my art, but it's never been enough. It'll always be a part of me, inside me, but I need something else, something

KISS AND RIDE

more, and I still don't know what that is. I guess I needed some sort of closure before I felt free enough to dream about the future." He swallowed thickly, then took a deep breath before aiming a small smile at Luca. "You've been my own Christmas miracle, you know? I couldn't have gone through all this without falling completely apart if it wasn't for you." He leaned in and Luca met him half way, kissing him gently. "And you need to keep fighting for your restaurant," he continued, his voice growing harder. "Don't let them win, baby. You fight those fuckers – no offence – till the end."

Luca laughed despite himself. "None taken." His voice sounded utterly defeated, and Vin felt it. His lips pressed into a determined line and he sat up, offering Luca his hand.

"Come on," he said to Luca's confusion.

"Come on, what?"

"Get dressed. We're going out," Vin declared already jumping off the bed.

"Out? It's 3 AM!"

"I don't care what time it is. I need to show you something."

After a mad dash through the quiet street of Rome, Vin nearly sprinting and pulling Luca behind him, they arrived at *Fontana di Trevi*, out of breath and panting. Luca forgot about his burning lungs the moment he laid eyes on the fountain. He'd never seen it completely empty, not a single tourist in sight. The noise of the falling water seemed louder, the sculptures sharper, and the colors bursting out of the water more vibrant.

Still confused, he turned to Vin to see him patting his pockets for something.

"Vin..." He said, trying to ask what this was all about, but Vin shushed him, taking his hand and leading him closer to the fountain. Luca felt the tiny droplets of water landing on his skin as he grabbed the railing and stared into the depths of the colorful water.

"Remember how I said now is not the right time for us?" Vin said, bringing Luca's attention back to him. Luca nodded, his brows pulling down. "I didn't mean that our time will never come. When I finish my degree I'll be able to live anywhere in the world, and when you get your restaurant you'll quit your job and finally settle in one place." Vin cut himself off, his bright blue eyes studying Luca as if trying to see if he'd said too much. Luca smiled at him, his heart thumping wildly in his chest. Vin's words were giving him hope, letting him know this wasn't the end. That he wasn't pulling Vin into his arms and kissing him silly for the last time. "This is not a goodbye, but I'm not asking you to wait for me either," Vin said when Luca released him. Luca opened his mouth to say something, but Vin put a finger to his lips, cutting him off. "But..." Vin swallowed hard, his eyes filling with tears. "But I want to keep in touch. I want to talk to you and text you stupid stuff and..." He lost the battle, a lone tear spilling down his cheek. Luca brushed it away with his thumb.

At that moment, there was no doubt in his mind that he'd fallen in love with this beautiful, talented, temperamental man, and he'd do anything in his power not to lose him.

"Vin, I..." Vin's eyes widened as if sensing Luca was about to say something big. Something there was no going back from.

"No!" He cut him off, placing a hand over his mouth. "Don't say it. Not now."

Luca wiggled away from Vin's hand. "Not saying it doesn't change how I feel."

"I know." Vin licked his lips, tucking his hand in his pockets. "Let's make a deal. On Christmas Eve next year, if you still feel that way, meet me right here. And say it then."

Taking his hand out of his pocket, Vin opened his palm and showed Luca a single coin. With a flick of his wrist he threw it into the fountain, watching it sink with a smile on his face.

"Now I have no choice but to come back to Rome," he said, his smile widening when Luca drew him in his arms again.

They spent the rest of the night sitting in front of the fountain, talking, watching the sky as it grew lighter. Neither of them seemed to want to move when Vin's phone started buzzing with the alarm he'd set to make sure he didn't miss his flight.

Traffic crept agonizingly slow. Vin sulked in the passenger seat while Luca drove, neither of them too keen to speak. It had been an emotional night, and considering they hadn't slept at all, talking required a lot of effort.

Luckily they'd left Luca's apartment with time to spare so Vin wasn't worried they'd be late, even in this traffic. His body couldn't handle the added stress. He'd never been this tired, this emotionally drained.

The car kept crawling at five miles per hour when Vin noticed the signs for the airport starting to appear. That meant they were getting closer. The urge to tell Luca to turn around and fuck everything, he was staying, was strong. But he knew all he'd said last night was true. It wasn't their time, not yet.

KISS AND RIDE

"'Kiss and Ride'? What's that?" Vin asked when his gaze landed on a road sign right under the 'Short Stay Car Park' for the airport.

"It's a drop off point," Luca said, glancing at Vin uncertainly. "You've never seen one before?"

Vin laughed, not entirely sure Luca wasn't kidding. "For real? Its actual name is Kiss and Ride? It's not some lost in translation thing?"

"Yes, it's the actual name."

"I'm already imaging an Italian stallion opening the door for me, lips puckered for a kiss. I won't be allowed out of the car if I don't give him a nice, long smooch."

Luca laughed, but there was an edge to his voice when he spoke. "I'm the only Italian stallion you'll be kissing today, *tesoro*."

God, Vin loved it when Luca called him that. Heat rose to his cheeks when his body reacted to Luca's words.

"So, wait, if that Kiss and Ride thing is the drop off point, we aren't in the right lane," Vin said, pointing at the road sign.

"I wasn't planning on dropping you off and speeding away." Luca clutched at the wheel tighter, a muscle jumping in his jaw. "I'll park at the car park and walk you to the terminal."

Vin released a slow exhale, wondering how to form his words so that they didn't offend Luca.

"I'd rather you dropped me off, Luca," he said quietly, his throat closing off around the words. He swallowed a few times before continuing. "This is hard enough. I don't want to kiss you goodbye and fall apart in front of everyone at the terminal."

Luca didn't reply, but he smoothly changed lanes until he was in the Kiss and Ride one.

A few minutes later, he was guiding the car into one of the drop off bays. Killing the engine, Luca turned in the seat to face Vin who unbuckled his seat belt and without a moment hesitation leaned in and kissed him. He didn't want to stop, didn't want to say goodbye.

"I never expected this when I came here," Vin said, resting his forehead against Luca's. "It's been intense and chaotic and ... wonderful. I wouldn't change a thing."

Luca cupped his cheek and kissed him again, his other hand clutching at Vin's shirt as if he never wanted to let him go.

Vin leaned back, meeting Luca's eyes. "If you meet someone else..." He began, but Luca closed his eyes in denial and cut him off.

"Vin..."

"No, listen. If you meet someone else, I don't want what could have been between us to stop you from what you can actually have with someone else."

"So, you'll be okay with me falling for someone else? Kissing him, making love to him, making breakfast for him every morning..." He said, his frown deepening with every word.

"No. I'll be climbing out of my skin with jealousy! But I want you to be happy."

Fuck, this was hard.

"Okay." Luca said, palming Vin's neck and bringing him down for another kiss. "I know I should probably say the same thing to you, but I can't." Luca puffed a heavy breath, his lower lip trembling a little. "The mere thought of someone... else being with you feels like I've taken a sledgehammer to my heart. But... I want you to be happy, too. Whatever it takes."

Vin kissed him again – one last time – before he opened the car door and stepped onto the pavement. Luca brought his luggage from the trunk, hugging him tightly, before turning and walking back to his car without a second glance.

Vin watched him as he drove away, clutching the handle of his suitcase, completely lost and alone in the world as the tears were finally allowed to fall down his cheeks.

January

Vin: I quit my job at the gallery and signed up for an Art Therapy course at NYU. I have a lot of free time now that I don't have to work and can probably do all the required courses much faster. ***crosses fingers***

Luca: That's great! Feels like a puzzle piece's fallen in place, you know? You'll be absolutely amazing at it.

Vin: Don't know about that... But it's really interesting and I love the idea of helping people through art.

Luca: I **know** you'll be great at it, I can feel it. Don't argue with my sixth sense.

Vin: Wouldn't dream of it.

Vin: So, where are you? I keep losing track of your destination.

KISS AND RIDE

Luca: Buenos Aires.

Vin: God, I'm jealous. The winter here's been brutal. I can use some sun. Send me a pic of you in speedos.

Luca: I'm not wearing speedos, but here's one of me drinking a Margarita in my shorts.

Vin: Fuck, you're gorgeous. I miss you so much

Luca: Miss you too, *amore*.

Vin: Stop being so fucking beautiful first thing in the morning!

Luca: I can't! It's the way I am, baby! Here, have another one.

Vin: Fuuuuuck, stop torturing meeeee!!! And put some clothes on.

Vin: Two can play that game.

Luca: I'd smack that delicious ass of yours if I was there. And then bite it. And then, if you're a good boy, stick my tongue in it.

Vin: Uuunnnnggggg

KISS AND RIDE

February

Vin: Any news from the lawyers?

Luca: Not really. The appeal is being submitted and now we wait for the court date.

Vin: Do you know how long that'll take?

Luca: No idea. Lawyer says it'll probably be months. All the fucking bureaucracy, man. Drives me nuts.

Vin: OK. Keep me posted. And let me know if there's anything I can do to help.

Luca: Thanks. But there isn't much anyone could do now. It's all up to the judge.

Luca: I'm so fucking tired of this, *tesoro*.

Vin: I know, baby. But you promised me you won't give up. Don't break that promise.

Luca: I won't.

KISS AND RIDE

March

Vin's phone rang just as he was about to give up on the assignment he'd been writing for most of the evening and go to bed. Shit, it was past midnight, again. Even without the added workload of having a full-time job, juggling two degrees at the same time wasn't easy. But Vin had a plan, and for that plan to work he needed to push himself harder than he ever had.

The sight of Luca's smiling face on the screen made his heart beat faster, both from excitement and worry. They rarely spoke on the phone because they were usually in vastly different time zones, so if Luca was calling without even texting first something must be wrong.

Hands shaking, Vin took the phone from his desk and slid his finger over the display.

"Hey, everything okay?"

Luca's melodic laughter filtered through the speakers. "Hey yourself." Vin heard some rustling before Luca spoke again. "Yeah, everything's fine. I just missed you."

Vin smiled, relaxing back into his chair. "I miss you, too."

Luca sighed, the sound amplified by the speaker. "I got home a few hours ago and I just... I'd much rather sleep in a different hotel every night than in my own bed. Everything here reminds me of you. It's been driving me crazy for the past couple of months."

Vin quickly calculated that it must be 6 AM in Rome right now, and Luca sounded wide awake as if he hadn't slept at all.

"Do you sleep?" Vin asked, knowing Luca's sleep patterns were different when he was working and when he was home. He wasn't a big sleeper, used to grab a few hours here and there between flights until he had a few days off to recuperate.

"Not much."

"I wish there was something I could do," Vin said, his body aching with the need to touch Luca, pull him and his arms and hold him until the world around them disappeared and it was just them.

"You are doing something. Hearing your voice helps."

So Vin kept talking. He told Luca about the assignment he was writing and about the new art project he was working on; about dinner with his friends the other night and seeing the latest blockbuster which had been very disappointing; about being sick of the cold weather and looking forward to spring and

KISS AND RIDE

summer when he could leave his apartment more often to study outside.

Luca didn't interrupt him. He hummed once in a while, but other than that he kept silent. By the time Vin ran out of things to say, he could hear Luca's soft snores coming from the other side.

"Night, baby," he whispered with a sad smile. Then, knowing Luca was asleep and couldn't hear him added, "Love you."

Luca called every night for the next three days. He was scheduled on a long flight to Bangkok on Monday, and then another one to Havana before he had a few days off again. Vin was worried Luca was working way too much, not giving his body time to recover from the long flights and the time difference. But just as Vin had taken on more than he could handle, he knew Luca was doing it for a reason. On one hand he needed the money, on the other it was easier to not think about missing each other when they were buried in work.

"What are you wearing?" Luca asked when Vin picked up.

Vin laughed, shaking his head. It was Sunday night and it was bittersweet hearing Luca's cheeky voice when he probably wouldn't be able to talk to him for weeks after tonight.

"A pink jockstrap and nothing much else," Vin purred.

He heard something crash and Luca swore away from the phone before coming back on the line.

"Really?" He sounded a little breathless but Vin wasn't sure if it was caused by his jockstrap comment or whatever he'd scrambled to pick up off the floor.

"No," Vin said with a laugh.

But then an idea struck him.

"Would you like me to?"

Luca inhaled sharply. "Good god, yes," he said, the last word followed by a little moan.

"Alright. Give me a sec."

He nearly ran to his bedroom, unearthing the pink jockstrap from the bottom of his underwear drawer and changing into it as quickly as he could. Then he lay on the bed, taking a few pictures of himself wearing it and sending them to Luca.

"God, I wish I was there right now," Luca said, his voice sounding different as if he'd switched to loudspeaker. Vin turned on his loudspeaker, too, placing the phone on his chest and freeing his hands.

KISS AND RIDE

"What would you do if you were here, hm?" Vin lowered his voice to a seductive purr, pleasure shooting through his body when he rubbed his already hard cock through the jockstrap.

"I'd kneel between your legs, mouth your cock through the fabric and tease you until you can't stand it anymore." Luca spoke slowly, his voice hoarse with pent up arousal. "Then I'll pull the jockstrap to the side exposing your beautiful, hard cock, and lick the precome from the tip."

Vin was going to explode. His body was taut with the effort of keeping himself from coming. And yet, he tortured himself by pulling his jockstrap aside, just as Luca'd said, and wrapping his fingers around his cock, slowly smearing the pearly drops from the tip.

"Would you like that, *carino*?"

"Fuck, yes," Vin managed to say before a loud, husky moan escaped his throat. "And then what?"

"And then I'll suck your cock all the way into my mouth, making it nice and wet for my ass."

Vin jerked, the phone sliding down from his chest onto the bed. Grabbing for it, he nearly disconnected the call before placing it back where it was.

"We haven't done that yet," he said slowly, his hand speeding on his shaft. The idea of fucking Luca had been popping into his head more and more often, sneaking into his fantasies and making him come harder than anything else.

"I've been thinking about it a lot," Luca said on the other end.

"Why didn't you say anything when we were together?"

"You needed it more than me."

That was true. In Rome, it hadn't even occurred to Vin to discuss this with Luca. He'd been more than happy to bottom, and Luca was right – he needed it back then. More than Luca would ever know.

"Do you need me now, baby?" Vin said, his voice growing playful again.

"Yes," Luca said with a sharp exhale.

"Do you have a dildo at hand?"

"No. But I have a butt plug."

Vin moaned, grabbing the base of his cock and squeezing. Imagining Luca spread open for him, butt plug inside him, nearly did him in.

"Get it," Vin commanded breathlessly. "And put it in."

Through the fog of lust currently clogging his brain, Vin heard some rustling noises and a few moments later Luca was back on the line.

"I'm getting myself ready for you, Vin," Luca said, his voice strained. "Fuuuuck."

"God, Luca, you're killing me." Vin's hand on his cock sped up, his concentration slipping away. "Tell me what you're doing."

"I'm playing with the butt plug, imagining it's you inside me," Luca said, voice hoarse with arousal. "I

KISS AND RIDE

need you so much, *carino*. I need you to touch me, kiss me, whisper how much you want me while you work that big cock inside me, making me see stars."

"I want that, too," Vin managed to say, but his voice was giving out on him. He was too deep under the haze of pleasure. Images of Luca thrusting the butt plug in and out of his ass, pinching his nipples, biting his lip, a drop of sweat running down his temple burst in vivid color in Vin's mind, and he couldn't hold back anymore.

With a hoarse cry he came all over the pink jockstrap, his body bowing off the bed as he panted, riding the last waves of his orgasm.

Vin reached for the phone that had fallen on the bed again, making sure the call hadn't disconnected. Taking it off speakerphone, he pressed it to his ear just in time to hear Luca calling out his name as he came.

"Luca?"

"Hm?"

Vin laughed. "That was... I've never done that before, but even without the prior experience I know that was fucking amazing."

"It really was," Luca sounded breathless and sleepy, and Vin could see him in his mind, sprawled on the bed they'd shared, his hair a tangled mess, his lips curved in a dreamy, lopsided smile.

"I wish I was there with you," Vin said, his voice catching.

"Me too, *tesoro*. Me, too."

April

To: Luca_Roma@yahoo.it
From: Vincent.alesi@gmail.com
Subject: First solo exhibition!!!!

Hi Luca,

Omg it's over! My first solo exhibition is over!!! I'm dead on my feet! Weeks of putting the final touches on every piece, obsessing over every detail, agonizing over the impressive guest list... And it's finally over!

It went well. I was in a haze all evening, unable to believe that all the people Angela'd invited actually turned up. Everyone wanted to meet me and talk to me, and I felt incredibly uncomfortable discussing every piece over and over again. Thank god for Angela! She can talk art all day, and she knows my pieces so well, and all I had to do was nod at all the appropriate places and let her take the reins.

I got asked about my dad a lot, which sucked. I didn't want to talk about him at all, not with total strangers, not when I don't know him that well myself.

Kiss and Ride

It feels wrong, you know? But what feels worse is questioning myself, wondering if every single piece in the exhibition was sold by the end of the night because of my dad's name, and not my talent.

I spoke to a few journalists and art critiques, too, and they'll send me their articles once they're published. I wonder if my dad's name will be mentioned as often as mine.

Anyway, enough about that. An artist always doubts themselves, I guess.

I'm proud of myself, though, and I'm grateful and humbled by the amazing response last night. I need to create, not for anyone else, but for me. And if someone else ends up loving my art, then that's an added bonus.

OK, I'm rambling. I'll stop now. I'm attaching a few photos from the event, hope you like them.

Oh, I nearly forgot! I heard back about my last assignment, the one I told you about? About the bipolar teenager for whom we all needed to submit a proposal for treatment through art therapy. One of the proposals they chose to actually try in his therapy course was mine!!! Honestly, that makes me even happier than selling out the whole gallery in three hours.

I miss you, Luca. So, so much! Call me when you get back, I want to hear your voice.

Yours,
Vin

May

To: Luca_Roma@yahoo.it
From: Vincent.alesi@gmail.com
Subject: I'm a Master of Fine Arts!!! Finally!!!

Hi Luca,

I gradated! Fucking finally! I still have to finish my art therapy program, but I got my Master's Degree today and that feels like the biggest fucking achievement of my entire life! I'm attaching a few photos from the graduation ceremony for you.

How are you? Last time we spoke feels like ages ago. Texts and emails are great – loved the photos from Thailand by the way, you looked so fucking hot I wanted to lick my screen. But I miss your voice. I miss you, period. I wish we could just drop everything and be together, now, not in six months...

Any word from the lawyers? I know I ask all the time but I'm so fucking tired of waiting! I can't even imagine how you must feel.

Yours,
Vin

KISS AND RIDE

June

Vin was trying to juggle a cup of coffee, his messenger bag and a giant art folder without dropping any of them when he heard his phone ringing. Well, tough luck. Whoever it was, they had to wait until Vin got to the gallery and dropped the art folder off.

Fifteen minutes later he had his hands free to check his phone. His heart nearly stopped when he saw it had been Luca who'd been calling, and he'd left a voicemail message.

Luca never left him any voicemail, ever.

Trying not to panic, Vin checked his messages, his legs nearly giving out when he heard Luca's voice.

"Hi, *amore*. Um..." There was a lot of noise around him, and it seemed like he was at an airport. "So, look, I know we agreed to meet at Christmas when hopefully we both will have our shit together, but Luisa – my colleague, remember? I told you about her, the one with the baby face that always tells the dirtiest jokes? Anyway. Luisa wanted to trade her Fiumicino – JFK line with someone, and when I heard about it I couldn't resist." Vin had never heard Luca so nervous before. He was rambling and talking a mile a minute, and Vin still had no idea what he was talking about. He knew Luca didn't fly to North America anymore, so it was unlikely he was here in New York right now. Wasn't it? "Fuck, I'm doing this all wrong." Luca took a deep breath. "I'm in New York. And I'd like to see you. I completely understand if you don't want to, or if you're seeing someone else, or... Whatever. I realize I dropped in here unannounced and..."

Was he being serious? Seeing someone else? What the actual fuck was he thinking?

Vin couldn't listen to him ramble anymore. He disconnected the call and dialedLuca's number. He picked up on the second ring.

"Hey."

"Seeing someone else? Are you for real? I can't think of anyone but you, I thought you knew that! My obsession with you is borderline illegal, and you think I may be seeing someone else? What the fuck is wrong with you?"

Luca laughed. He fucking laughed. The throaty sound sinking into Vin's mind, imprinting on it, making his heart soar.

"I'm sorry. I never actually thought that, but..."

"But nothing!" Vin interrupted him. "Are you really here? In New York?"

"Yes. Landed at JFK half an hour ago. I have a three day layover and wanted to see you."

KISS AND RIDE

"Don't move. I'm coming to get you," Vin said, already raising a hand to signal a cab.

"You don't have to... I can get a taxi and meet you somewhere..."

"I'm coming to get you and we're spending the next three days in my bed. Got it?"

A cab pulled over and Vin jumped in it, telling the driver to drive to JFK and hurry up.

"Yes, sir," Luca said, amused.

"See? I like you much better when you're being reasonable."

The door hadn't even closed behind them when they were in each other's arms, kissing, pulling frantically at their clothes. Vin had wanted to do that the moment he'd seen Luca at the airport, looking sexy as hell in his cabin crew uniform. He'd barely restrained himself in the cab, but now that they were inside his apartment all bets were off.

Blindly, he backed Luca towards the bedroom, falling on top of him when they reached the bed.

They'd shed their clothes on the way, only their socks and pants remaining. Vin's hands roamed greedily over Luca's body, he was unable to get enough of him.

Six months. Six months he'd imagined this moment, and now he couldn't slow down enough to enjoy it.

Fuck that. Time for slow later. Now he needed to be inside Luca as much as he needed his next breath.

"Couldn't stop thinking about you and the butt plug," Vin murmured in Luca's ear, biting the earlobe. Luca grunted underneath him, too far gone for words. "I want to fuck you, baby. So damn much I can't stand it."

"Do it." Luca was breathless, his skin damp, his body already trembling with anticipation.

Vin kissed him again, rough and demanding, biting his lips, his tongue exploring every crevice of Luca's mouth.

"I'll be right back," he said, tearing himself away from Luca with great effort.

He shucked his pants and socks on the way to the bathroom, grabbing a bunch of condoms and the bottle of lube from the cabinet. When he got back to the bedroom, Luca had discarded his own underwear and was lying on his stomach, his head cradled in the crook of his arm, looking at Vin under his lashes.

He was gorgeous, so fucking sexy, and so irresistible that Vin never stood a chance. From the moment they'd met Vin had been a goner.

KISS AND RIDE

"Is that how you want it?" Vin whispered in Luca's ear as he settled on top of him, his hard cock settling against Luca's ass.

Luca nodded, a throaty, needy moan escaping him as he pushed his ass back against Vin. Biting his shoulder, Vin smacked his ass and leaned back on his haunches, making quick work of the condom and slicking them both up. He lowered himself on top of Luca, supporting his weight on his forearms as he slid inside him. Luca groaned, and Vin gave him a minute to adjust, resting his forehead between Luca's shoulder blades.

Luca pushed back against him, silently urging Vin to move. It was hard, so fucking hard to control himself, make this as good for Luca as it was for him.

"Don't try to be gentle," Luca said, his voice thick. "I don't need you to be gentle right now."

Vin pulled back, wrapping an arm around Luca's waist and hosting him up on all fours. Hands palming Luca's ass, Vin watched his cock disappear in Luca's body, then slide back out. It was hypnotic, and so fucking hot that Vin thought he might combust if he didn't pick up the speed. Experimentally, he thrust his hips harder, and Luca cried out, dipping his spine and reaching for his cock.

"Do that again," he panted, jerking his cock in rhythm with Vin's thrusts.

Vin slammed into him, over and over, until he felt Luca's ass clench around him as he came with a tortured grunt. Vin pushed him back down on the bed, moving in a frantic rhythm, unable to hold back. His arms gave out when he came, and he fell on top of Luca, still rocking against him, slower, deeper, milking the last drop of pleasure from his cock.

***

"I love your tattoos," Luca said, tracing the ink on Vin's chest. "I want to get one. On my back."

"What do you want to get?" Vin caught Luca's hand in his and kissed it, entwining their fingers on his chest. They were so spent that they couldn't even bother with taking a shower or change the sheets. Luca had scooted on Vin's side of the bed, away from the wet spot, and they'd curled around each other, unwilling to fall asleep despite their exhaustion. Vin didn't want to waste a second of his time with Luca with sleep.

"I don't know exactly," Luca said, lifting his shoulder in a shrug. "I wanted to get my grandparents' initials woven into something pretty. But I haven't seen anything I like yet."

"What were their names?"

KISS AND RIDE

"Gianluca and Elena."

"I can do a design for you."

Luca lifted his head to meet Vin's eyes. "Really?"

"Of course."

Luca pushed forward, kissing Vin's lips tenderly. "I'd love that," he murmured against Vin's mouth, before deepening the kiss, and Vin forgot what they were talking about.

Luca didn't want to go sightseeing or do anything else but spend the entire three days they had in Vin's bed. He'd been to New York a dozen times, he'd seen and done nearly everything, but even if it'd been his first time in the city he'd still want to spend it wrapped in his romantic cocoon with Vin.

They ordered food and had sex, taking a break to nap or watch some TV. And they talked. About anything and everything that came to mind. When Vin'd left Rome six months ago Luca had been afraid that their feelings for each other would fizzle out, and they'd naturally drift apart. If anything, exactly the opposite had happened. He'd never felt this close to anyone, this in sync. Their connection had grown deeper, more intense, more *real* in their time apart.

"I want to show you something," Vin said suddenly, jostling Luca as he made to sit up.

"Is it the pink jockstrap?" Luca waggled his eyebrows. Vin bit his lip but his cheeks still dimpled when he shook his head. "If that something is anywhere out of this room, I'm not going," Luca pouted dramatically, crossing his arms.

"Come on. I really need you to see this, Luca."

With a loud groan, Luca sat up and headed to the bathroom. "This better be fucking good," he mumbled on the way, closing the door behind him.

Vin took him to a building a few blocks away from his apartment in Chelsea. He produced a key for the main door, and then another set of keys for the apartment on the top floor. He paused before pushing the door open.

"Nobody but me has ever been here before," he said, biting his lower lip nervously. "But I wanted to show you, because... Well, you'll see."

They walked into a converted loft, a huge open space with floor to ceiling windows without any blinds or curtains. The furniture was scarce – a large sofa against one wall, a small table with a lamp next to it, and a bookcase housing a disarray of various books, magazines, and notebooks.

KISS AND RIDE

The rest of the space was filled with paintings and art materials piled in every corner, easels, a pottery wheel, and boxes overflowing with supplies stacked against the walls. Luca had an uncomfortable flashback to Antonio's apartment, but unlike his studio, Vin's was lacking any of the suffocating madness. It was bright and airy, a place where he exercised his talent, not fell victim to it.

Vin closed the door and locked it, then passed by Luca and walked further inside. Luca followed him to one of the stack of paintings propped against the wall. They seemed like a series of four paintings, same technique, complementary colors, and even though they were done in a very abstract style Luca thought he could see a figure forming from the skewed shapes. Something about the paintings spoke to him, drew him in, and he couldn't look away.

"It's you," Vin said quietly, his eyes on the paintings. "I made that first one the day after we had phone sex for the first time." He pointed to the painting on the far right.

It all made sense now. As Luca studied the paintings, he saw the figure on all of them was naked, body twisted in pleasure. Goosebumps erupted on Luca's skin as he remembered that night, the longing he'd felt so accurately captured in these paintings.

"They're incredible," he said, wrapping an arm around Vin's waist and kissing his temple, his gaze still locked on the paintings.

Vin nodded, then buried his face in Luca's neck. They stayed like this – Luca staring at the paintings, Vin snuggled in his arms – for a long time before Vin showed him the rest of the art in the studio.

"These are all for me," he said, spreading his arms wide. "I've selected a few I can exhibit," he pointed to a small cluster of paintings and a clay sculpture. "But everything else feels too private the show the world."

Luca understood. Even if Vin's style was abstract, he managed to capture raw emotion in his art. Anyone who looked at it would know they were witnessing an intimate moment in Vin's life, even if they weren't sure exactly what it was.

They stayed in the studio for a while longer, Vin showing Luca his favorite pieces and explaining what inspired him. Lots of them were created right after he came back from Rome, the loneliness he must have felt clearly etched in them.

Later, in Vin's bed, he grew quiet, melancholic, laying on top of Luca, his head over Luca's heart, listening, his long lashes tickling Luca's skin when he blinked. It was their last night together and it could be another six months before they saw each other again. Every fiber in Luca's body was telling him he couldn't last that long, he couldn't keep working himself into mindless exhaustion just so that he didn't think of Vin that often. Didn't miss him.

KISS AND RIDE

"I have two weeks holiday I haven't used yet," Luca said, palms absently rubbing Vin's back. "How about I take the time off in July and you come stay with me in Rome?"

Vin took a deep breath, his chest rising and falling, but he didn't otherwise move. "I can't. I was going to call you this weekend to tell you that Professor Holman managed to get me a summer internship in an art therapy clinic in Chicago. I'm supposed to leave next week and I'm coming back last week of August."

Luca's stomach bottomed out. He felt weightless, and falling all at the same time. Vin must have sensed his unease because he lifted his head to look at him, the sadness Luca felt mirrored in his blue eyes. But there was something else. Resignation?

It's not the right time for us.

Vin's words echoed in Luca's head, and they'd never seemed more true.

"Hey," Vin said, reaching out to cup Luca's cheek. "It's just a few more months, right? I'm taking as many courses as I can and I should be done with most of the classes by December. I'll still have assignments to submit, but I can do that online from anywhere in the world, or come back for a week or two if I absolutely must." Luca felt himself nod, but the desperate sadness inside him didn't lift. Despite Vin's words he felt like they were saying goodbye. "And by then you should know for sure the outcome of the appeal. One way or another we'll make it work. Together."

Luca sighed, not sure what he'd do if his parents won the appeal. If he lost his restaurant, his *dream*. He had some money saved, but they wouldn't be enough if he had to start his restaurant from scratch somewhere else.

"Luca, listen to me," Vin said, rolling off him and propping his head on his elbow next to Luca. "You remember when Maria said Dad named me after Van Gogh because he thought I'd be one of the greats?" Luca nodded, their meeting with Maria as vivid in his mind as if it'd happened yesterday. "I don't want that. I don't want to be a slave of my art, turning into a recluse who pushes everyone away. I want to have a life full of people I care about, a life that means something other than some pretty paintings." Vin swallowed, his Adam's apple working, his blue eyes glazing over. "I want a life with you."

Luca closed his eyes, letting Vin's words penetrate every cell in his body until they were ingrained in his DNA.

He wanted that, too. God, he craved it. And Vin deserved to know that, even if it didn't turn out this way, even if they did drift apart in the next few months, he deserved to know how Luca felt.

"I want that too," he finally said. "Before, I used to day dream about my restaurant, what it would look like, designing the menu in my head over and over,

KISS AND RIDE

imagining the decor, the people, the noise in the kitchen..." Luca leaned in and kissed Vin gently, lingering for a few seconds before pulling away. "Ever since I met you the reality of my day dreams has changed. I still see my restaurant, still believe it'll eventually happen, but now I see you, too. Everywhere I turn you're there, helping me with the food choices or smiling at me from across the room or helping the interior designer because I suck at that kinda thing." Vin was smiling at him, and it gave Luca the courage to continue. "I know that's not your dream. It's mine and I inserted you in there without even asking. But..." Luca's throat closed off, and embarrassingly enough his eyes filled with tears. "But I love you, and I want to be with you, no matter where, no matter what we do."

Vin grinned at him, losing the battle with his own tears as they rolled down his cheeks.

"I love you, too," he said, before kissing Luca, a wet, tear drenched kiss that felt like a promise. "And I want all this, too," he whispered against Luca's lips, holding him close, not letting him pull away. "I don't care where we end up as long as we're together. And I *know* we can make it work."

As Vin kissed him again, Luca wished, harder than he'd ever wished for anything, that Vin's words were true.

TEODORA KOSTOVA

July

To: Luca_Roma@yahoo.it
From: Vincent.alesi@gmail.com
Subject: Arrived in Chicago

Hi Luca,

Just arrived at the apartment in Chicago. The internship starts on Monday so I have the entire weekend to explore the city. I'll send you some pics later.

I'm really excited about this. I have no idea what to expect, and I'm nervous as hell, but excited! It'll be tough – I'm scheduled to work ten hour days, six days a week, and I have a few assignments to complete and submit in September if I want to have any chance of graduating before December, but I'll manage. I know I will.

What I said before... It's all true, Luca. You seemed so disheartened when you left, it broke my heart. I don't want you to be sad, baby. We'll get

KISS AND RIDE

through this, I promise you. I'll be at *Fontana di Trevi* on Christmas Eve, and it'll be romantic as fuck.

And I'll be all yours, for as long as you want me.

Love you so much.
Yours,
Vin

August

Vin: Fuck, I'm tired. I want to sleep for a week.

Luca: You got back home?

Vin: Yeah, just landed. Waiting for my luggage.

Luca: Let's Skype later. I just arrived in Tokyo and should have decent internet connection at the hotel.

Vin: OK, babe. Talk later. X

KISS AND RIDE

When Luca's face appeared on Vin's laptop screen he couldn't help but beam at him. Touching the screen with the tips of his fingers – fingerprints be damned – he felt tears prickling behind his eyes. He missed Luca so much it was hard to breathe sometimes, the longing in his chest expanding and growing heavier until it nearly crushed his insides.

"Hey," Vin said, trying to compose himself. He wasn't going to cry, not fucking again.

"Hi, *tesoro*," Luca said, blowing a kiss at the camera.

The image was quite good, not as grainy as it usually was when Luca was on the other side of the world, trying to make the most of a free WiFi connection. Vin frowned when he saw the dark circles under Luca's eyes, exhaustion clearly written on his face. His high cheekbones were even more prominent now, as if he'd lost weight. Vin tried to remember when was the last time he'd seen any pictures of Luca, and came up with a single photo right after Luca'd gone back to Rome in June. Since then, they'd emailed and texted, called a few times but they'd both been so busy it'd been hard to synchronize their schedules, and the time difference was always in the way.

"How are you?" Vin asked, hoping Luca would be honest and they could talk about why he looked like shit.

"I'm good," he said instead, giving Vin a tired smile. "How was the internship?"

Vin'd texted him a few bits and pieces about his summer job, and emailed him some photos, but they hadn't talked about it at length. He wasn't too happy with the change of subject – he still wanted to ask Luca why he wasn't sleeping and why he was obviously taking more work that he could handle, but he refrained. Luca looked exhausted enough to keel over, and Vin didn't want to stress him even more.

So, he told him about the internship. His heart beat faster every time Luca smiled at him, happiness blooming on his tired face.

"It was so amazing to see how art can actually help people. How it's not just something pretty to look at, you know?"

Luca nodded with a yawn. Poor guy looked dead on his feet.

"Have you heard anything from the lawyers?" Vin asked, hope erupting in his chest when Luca visibly brightened.

"Yes! This morning. The court date is set for October."

"Fucking finally," Vin said with an eye roll.

"Can't rush bureaucracy." Another yawn tore out of Luca, and Vin decided it was time to let him rest.

"It'll be okay," he said, and Luca smiled at him but his slight nod wasn't very convincing. "Whatever happens, I'll be at the fountain on Christmas Eve."

Luca looked away.

You'll be there, too. Right?

KISS AND RIDE

Vin didn't voice that thought. He couldn't. He had to believe Luca hadn't changed his mind, or his entire world would crumble under his feet. And he wasn't ready for that.

September

Luca: Some asshole set himself on fire on the plane. We're all fine but had to make an emergency landing in Moscow. Hope I didn't wake you, I know it's like 3 AM in New York right now, but I knew you'd probably read about it on Twitter or something when you woke up and didn't want you to worry.

Vin read the text, blinking rapidly as the bright light from the display assaulted his bleary eyes. His heart hammered in his chest as he dialled Luca's number.

"Luca?" He said, sitting up in the bed.

"Hi, *carino*," Luca sounded tired. "I'm sorry, I didn't want to wake you but we're scheduled to depart in an hour and I'll be in the air for the next few hours."

"Forget about that." Vin waved a hand in front of his face. "Tell me what happened."

"I don't really know, to be honest. I was answering a call from row eighteen when this guy a few

KISS AND RIDE

rows back started screaming. I looked at him and saw he was frantically waving his hands around and they were on fire!"

"Jesus Christ!"

"At first I thought his phone had burst into flames, but when I reached him I saw the lighter on the floor. He tried to grab me, but I managed to avoid him, and then Franco was running, holding a fire extinguisher. By then the whole plane was in panic, people were screaming, it was a fucking mess! We got a hold of the situation, eventually, managed to restrain the guy who seemed to be having some sort of a mental breakdown and kept screaming about how fire will set us all free or some such nonsense."

Luca sighed heavily, and Vin's heart sank. What he wouldn't give to be with him right now.

"That sounds really scary, Luca. I'm so glad you're okay."

Vin's imagination conjured images of a plane bursting into flames high in the sky, plummeting down, people screaming for the last time before they all died. His mind filled with bright red shapes and his fingers started to itch.

"I'm fine, but we're all a bit shaken. We're trained to handle all sorts of unpredictable situations, but this was just..." He sighed again, cutting himself off.

A loud voice announced something in Russian, and Vin had to pull the phone away from his ear.

"I have to go," Luca said when the tinny voice from the speakers was done. "I'll text you when I land in Beijing."

"Okay," Vin said, wanting to say so much more, but their time was cut short, again. "Love you."

"Love you, too."

Vin knew his mind wouldn't let him rest anymore, so he got up, pulled some random clothes on and headed for his studio.

KISS AND RIDE

October

Luca: I fucking WON!!!!!

Vin: OMG!!! Really?? It's over?? The house is yours?

Luca: YES

Vin: They can't appeal again, or come up with something else?

Luca: NO

Vin: That's the best news EVER! I'm so so happy for you, babe! I love you so much!!!

Luca: Love you, too, *tesoro*. Can't wait to take you to the house!

Vin: Can't wait to see it! When are you quitting your fucking job? Have I told you how much I hate it?

Luca: Many times. I'll do as many flights as I can till December and then I'm giving my two weeks' notice. I also have 2 weeks holiday I haven't used, so I think I'm going to use it next month to go see the house. I need to meet with the lawyers, too, iron out any last details.

Vin: Do you want me to come with you to Sicily?

Luca: No. You have to submit your last two assignments, remember? You can't afford to miss any classes.

Vin: You know I'll be there if you need me, right?

Luca: I know, and I love you so much for that, but I can do this on my own. Besides, I want you to be done with school when you come here in December. Once I have you in my arms again I'm not letting you go.

KISS AND RIDE

November

Vin heard his phone ringing and raced to the living room. He was expecting Luca to call once he got to the house and couldn't wait to hear his excited voice when he saw his grandparents' house for the first time in years.

"Hey!" Vin panted in the speaker, nearly falling down as he tripped over the carpet. "Did you make it to Cefalù?"

Luca didn't immediately reply and Vin looked at the phone to make sure the connection wasn't lost.

"Luca?"

He heard a heavy sigh, or maybe it was a strangled sob, from the other end, but nothing much else.

"Luca? What the hell is going on? Are you okay?" Vin's voice kept rising with each word, panic settling in.

"I'm fine," Luca said, his voice a hoarse whisper.

"You're scaring me, baby. Talk to me. What happened?"

"It's trashed. All of it. The whole house is trashed, Vin. There isn't much left."

"What? But... How? Who would do such a thing?"

Luca laughed bitterly. "If I had to bet my last cent on someone it would be my parents."

"Your parents? Are you serious?"

"I guess they didn't do it themselves, but there are enough people who can do that for the right price."

Vin heard some noises as if Luca was walking around, picking stuff and then dropping it down.

"Didn't anyone see? Why didn't the police call you?"

"The house is outside of the village, there're no neighbors around. I guess nobody heard anything. And besides, it looks fine on the outside. I didn't know anything was wrong before I pushed the door open."

"How bad is it?" Vin asked, holding his breath for Luca's reply.

"It's bad, *carino*. Really, really bad. All the furniture is broken, there're holes in the walls, electric cables poking out. The hardwood floors are ripped out, and there's mold everywhere as if the place had been flooded. I'm surprised they didn't burn the whole thing down."

Vin couldn't begin to imagine the hatred someone must carry inside them to do such a thing to their own child, if Luca's guess was right. But who else could it be? Random vandalism or robbery wouldn't do such irreparable damage.

"Is the house insured?" Vin asked.

"No. I wanted to insure it, but I couldn't until it was legally mine. Guess who knew that tiny bit of information."

"Fucking assholes!" Vin swore, so fucking angry he could strangle Luca's parents if he ever saw them. Taking a deep breath, he said, "I'm coming down there. We're going to figure this whole thing out together."

"No, Vin, don't do that. Don't throw away everything we've worked so hard for this year. Finish your course, submit all your work so that you know that chapter of your life is done." Luca sounded so fucking resigned that Vin wanted to scream. "Besides, there isn't much you can do here. I'm going to get someone in tomorrow to do basic repairs and make sure the house is safe, and then lock it up and go back home. I'll probably need to sell some of the land to get enough money to fix all this damage, and I can't deal with it right now."

Alarm bells sounded in Vin's mind. Sell some of the land? But what if some big corporation bought it and turned it into a mall? Or something equally disruptive to the idyllic countryside?

"Okay, let's make a deal. I'll stay here and finish my course, and you'll promise not to sell anything until I get there," Vin said.

"I promise."

KISS AND RIDE

December

Vin: Submitted my last assignment!!! I'm a free man!

Luca: Awesome! Now get your perky ass down here.

Vin: 2 days, baby. 2 more days and I'm all yours.

Vin: At the airport. See you in a few hours.

TEODORA KOSTOVA

Luca paced in front of the fountain, unable to sit still for longer than a few seconds, its beauty completely lost on him tonight. It was in the middle of the night and he'd been waiting for two hours, and there was still no sign of Vin. He'd tried calling so many times, but always got his voicemail; tried texting but the texts remained unread. Worry ate at him, making him check the news channels on his phone obsessively for anything unusual that might have delayed him.

He'd checked Vin's flight and it had landed three hours ago. It should have only taken Vin about an hour to get here. And why was his phone switched off?

What if he'd simply changed his mind?

His brain tried to feed him some rational thoughts like, *Vin loves you, he'd never do that*, and, *He texted you from the airport*, but Luca wasn't listening. All he knew was that he'd never wanted anything more than he wanted Vin, and right now it felt like that dream of them building a life together was crashing and burning all around him.

KISS AND RIDE

Luca was starting to think that the universe was playing with him, giving him what he wanted simply to take it all away a moment later.

Church bells chimed from two different directions. 2 AM. Luca tried calling again. Voicemail.

With a heavy sigh, he sat on the edge of the fountain, despair wrapping itself around him until he was lost inside it. Dropping his head in his hands, Luca didn't know what to do. Didn't know what to think. Just didn't fucking *know*.

In the quiet of the night, all he could hear was the water splashing in the fountain and... Was that footsteps? Luca jumped to his feet, spinning in a circle, trying to see where the footsteps were coming from.

And then he saw him. Vin. Coming out from one of the side streets, tripping over his feet as he hurried towards Luca.

Luca met him half way, enveloping him in his arms with no intention of ever letting go.

"You're here," he said, cupping Vin's face in his cold hands. "You're really here."

Vin frowned. "Of course I am. Did you think for one second I wasn't going to come?" His eyes widened when Luca looked away. "You asshole!" Vin exclaimed, hitting Luca on the arm. "How can you not trust me by now?"

"I do trust you." Vin raised an eyebrow in challenge. "I just thought that maybe you changed your mind. Maybe this isn't what you really want, maybe..."

"Fucking shut up and kiss me."

Luca did. He kissed Vin as if he was kissing him for the first time. His lips were cold, and so were his hands in Luca's hair, on his neck, on his cheeks, but Luca didn't care. He'd have kissed Vin in a blizzard.

"What happened?" Luca asked, forcing himself to pull away, but not entirely letting go of Vin. "And where's your luggage?" Vin's messenger bag hung off his off his shoulder but he had no suitcase with him.

Vin rolled his eyes. "I'm just not made for travel. Every time I attempt it everything goes wrong." He leaned in and kissed Luca again, as if he couldn't stand to not kiss him. "The plane was delayed in New York, then when we landed in Rome we waited ages for our luggage. My fucking phone was dead and after emptying my entire bag on my seat, I realized I'd left my charger in the suitcase.

"And then, of course, my luggage never appeared on the belt. I waited for like an hour for someone from the airline help desk to trace my suitcase and give me a reference number. They're supposed to deliver it tomorrow, but since it's Christmas I highly doubt that." Luca was smiling. He couldn't help it. He'd missed Vin so damn much even his story of unfortunate events made him smile. "And then I went to the apartment first but you weren't there so I had to get another taxi here."

KISS AND RIDE

"Why would you do that? You wanted a romantic meeting in front of the fountain on Christmas Eve!"

Vin's smile dimpled his cheeks, his blue gaze holding Luca's like a willing hostage.

"I'm an artist. I need everything to be incredibly dramatic," he said with an expressive eye roll. "But I didn't think you'd wait for me here that long in the cold."

"I'd wait for you, for as long as it takes, *amore*," Luca said, pulling Vin in for a kiss. "Always."

Vin kissed him back eagerly, but Luca could feel his smile underneath the kiss.

"Let's go home," Luca murmured as he nuzzled Vin's jaw. "I'm freezing."

"Okay, but I need to do something first." Vin pulled away, holding Luca's gaze and biting his lip as if uncertain of what he was about to do.

Luca arched an eyebrow, curious what Vin had in mind. Letting go of Luca, Vin moved towards the fountain, turning his back on it when he reached the railing. With a cheeky smile he dug into his coat's pocket, finding whatever he needed with ease. Still holding Luca's gaze, Vin threw a coin in the fountain over his shoulder, then another one, and then a third one. His grin was so wide it made his cheeks dimple.

Luca's heart was beating so fast he thought it might explode. Crooking a finger in Vin's direction,

Luca beckoned him over, and Vin didn't hesitate before running back into Luca's arms.

KISS AND RIDE

December

4 years later

Sofia, Vin's twelve year old patient, was painting quietly beside him. She was always quiet. Her parents had thought art therapy would be good for her because she loved drawing, and sketching in her notebook was the only thing that made her smile.

Vin had been seeing her once a week for six months, and about a month ago she'd started humming to herself as she painted. Sofia loved colors. She was great with the charcoal, too, but give her some acrylic paints and her personality really started shining through.

During their sessions, Vin would sit next to her in front of his own easel, and as he painted, he'd talk to her about anything that came to mind. With the corner of his eye he watched for any reaction. She'd pause, brush poised mid-air when she was really engrossed in his story, or wrinkle her nose when Vin was being silly, or smile widely when he said something funny.

After the session, Vin walked Sofia to the door, waving at her mother waiting for her in the car outside.

"Merry Christmas, Sofia," he said, smiling at her. "Hope you have a lovely time during the holidays."

Something flickered in her eyes before she tucked a stand of dark hair behind her ear and said,

"You, too." Blushing, she jogged down the steps and to her mother's car.

Vin grinned widely. That was the first time in six months the girl had said anything to him, and according to her parents, she didn't speak at home either. They were making progress and he couldn't be happier.

Back inside his clinic, Vin went about tidying everything away. Sofia had been his last patient before the holidays, and he wanted to make sure everything was in order before they left for Rome tomorrow.

Folding the easels away, Vin looked out the window. The sun was setting, casting an orange glow over their house and Luca's restaurant across the field. Four years ago he'd purchased half of Luca's land and built his art therapy clinic on it. Luca had been against it, at first, thinking that Vin was doing it only as a way of giving him money to restore the house and rebuild the restaurant adjacent to it. But Vin managed to convince him that wasn't true, hiring an architect to make plans for the building of the clinic and presenting them to Luca.

He'd caved. He would have caved eventually, even without the clinic, and they both knew it. Vin had fantastic powers of persuasion.

Smiling to himself, Vin finished putting everything in order, made sure all the lights were turned off, and left the clinic, locking the door behind him. Their house was a five minute walk across the field – best commute to work ever. He absolutely loved living in Cefalù. It was beautiful and peaceful, and exactly what Vin needed.

He found Luca typing away on his laptop in the kitchen.

"Hey," he said, wrapping his arms around Luca's chest and bending down to kiss him. "Aren't you done yet?"

"Nearly. Give me ten minutes, okay?" Luca turned his head to meet Vin's lips in a lingering kiss.

"Okay," Vin said with a sigh. "But hurry up. I'd love some company in the shower."

Luca groaned and Vin thought he heard him hitting the keys a little bit faster.

Smiling to himself, Vin climbed the stairs to their bedroom and fell on the bed. He was so glad it was nearly Christmas and they could finally spend more time together. Ever since they'd moved to Cefalù four years ago, they'd made it a tradition to go to Rome for two weeks every Christmas. They stayed in Antonio's apartment, and it was amazing how year after year Vin kept discovering new things about his dad.

Maria always invited them for Christmas dinner, making the trip even more special. Vin's aunt was an extraordinary woman and Vin had grown to love and respect her.

Sitting up, Vin started undressing, a hot shower exactly what he needed after the long day he'd had. A hot shower with Luca – even better. Vin heard him moving around the kitchen, so he should be up soon.

In the past four years Luca had worked tirelessly to get his restaurant going. Currently, *Gianluca's* was popular with tourists and locals alike, everyone appreciating the delicious food and relaxed atmosphere. Luca had obsessed over the menu, testing his grandfather's recipes a million times, trying new ingredients to complement the old recipes, and always buying fresh, in-season produce from local farms. And it had paid off. *Gianluca's* was making profit before the end of the first year.

Luca had to hire additional staff, including a manager and a head chef, his business growing too fast for him to do everything himself. The manager, Alessandro, had been a godsend. He was young, with a degree in hospitality management, and very business savvy. He'd been on top of things from day one, and the restaurant ran like a well-oiled machine even when Luca wasn't there.

KISS AND RIDE

Alessandro had also suggested Luca start a blog, sharing his experience as a restaurant owner, and also recipes he'd come up with, and any sort of cooking advice. Luca's Kitchen had become so popular last year that Luca got offered a book deal. The cooking and lifestyle book named after his blog should be out next week, in time for Christmas.

These days Luca could be seen in front of the computer more often than in the kitchen, but he seemed to love it. Cooking was still his passion, but with the restaurant doing so well and having people he could trust to run it, he was free to do other things.

Like, take two weeks off during the holidays to spend them in Rome with Vin. Or four weeks in summer when he closed the restaurant for the entire month of August, let the staff enjoy their summer with paid vacation time, and travelled with Vin all over the world. Vin was still a disaster when it came to travelling – something always went wrong – but he loved discovering new, beautiful places and sharing these moments with the love of his life.

Vin finished undressing, dropping his clothes in the hamper. His eyes were drawn to the painting above their bed – The Girl and the Rain. His father's most famous painting hung in his bedroom and he wouldn't have it any other way. Their whole house was decorated with Antonio and Vin's art, their paintings hanging side by side, some of them too personal to be revealed to the world.

The art in the house alone cost a fortune, and Vin had a lot more stored away. He'd sold some of it to private collectors and donated to galleries around the world, but he'd kept the more personal ones, the ones that seemed to show a glimpse of Antonio's soul.

Not having to ever worry about money anymore had freed them both to do what they loved without always considering the cost first. Vin was free to paint, whenever he felt like it or not at all; Luca was free to run his restaurant as he saw fit, pay his staff generously as they deserved, and buy quality produce despite the higher price, even if that meant declaring smaller profit at the end of the year.

Vin walked naked into the en-suite bathroom, starting the water in the shower and letting it warm up. He thought he heard the bedroom door opening, and soon enough, Luca joined him in the bathroom, naked and grinning as he came to wrap his arms around Vin.

Vin ran his hands along Luca's back, mesmerized by the sight as he watched their reflection in the mirror. The muscles on Luca's broad back flexed and moved under his skin, making the tattoo on his back come alive. The elegant lines weaved around the letters E and G, connecting them, making them a part of something bigger, something beautiful and full of color. The bright light in the bathroom reflected in Vin's gold wedding band, making it sparkle like stardust against the olive skin on Luca's back.

KISS AND RIDE

"Missed you today," Luca said, pulling slightly back to kiss Vin's forehead. Vin'd left the house early, eager to finish a sculpture he'd been working on before Sofia's session. He hadn't even come to the house for lunch, and Luca had sent Alessandro to check on him and bring him something to eat. "Did you have a good day?"

Vin smirked, reaching behind Luca to grab his ass.

"It just got considerably better."

THE END

TEODORA KOSTOVA

ABOUT THE AUTHOR

Hi, my name is Teodora and I live in London with my husband and my son. I've been writing ever since I can remember, but it became my full time job in 2010 when I decided that everything else I've tried bores me to death and I have to do what I've always wanted to do, but never had the guts to fully embrace. I've been a journalist, an editor, a personal assistant and an interior designer among other things, but as soon as the novelty of the new, exciting job wears off, I always go back to writing. Being twitchy, impatient, loud and hasty are not qualities that help a writer, because I have to sit alone, preferably still, and write for most of the day, but I absolutely love it. It's the only time that I'm truly at peace and the only thing I can do for more than ten minutes at a time - my son has a bigger attention span than me. When I'm procrastinating, I like to go to the gym, cook Italian meals (and eat them), read, listen to rock music, watch indie movies and True Blood re-runs. Or, in the worst case scenario, get beaten at every Nintendo Wii game by a very inventive kid.

KISS AND RIDE

CONTACTS

www.facebook.com/teodorakostovaauthor

www.teodorakostova.blogspot.com

t.t.kostova@gmail.com

@Teodora_Kostova

ALSO BY TEODORA KOSTOVA

West End series

Dance

Mask

Dreaming of Snow

Piece by Piece

Snowed In

Cookies

Heartbeat series

In a Heartbeat

Then, Now, Forever

Printed in Great Britain
by Amazon